Praise for Marguerite Mooers' novels

"Take My Hand is a very good read--a well constructed mystery with an appealing detective reconstructing the scene and possible suspects of a 'cold case' child abduction. Mooers constructs the pieces of her puzzle nicely with an ultimately persuasive but not immediately obvious solution." Amazon review.

"The tension of "Take My Hand" really builds from the moment the detectives start investigating and does not let up---no easy feat for a procedural like this. Lorna is a great secondary character, with a well-developed emotional arc and compelling relationships that make her involvement in the case even more tense and dangerous." Writers Digest 23rd Self-Published Book Awards

"An amazing first book. The characters were real. Fast moving so I never lost interest in the plot. " Amazon review

"Marguerite Mooers Is a talented writer whose characters will send your heart pounding with fear and your palms sweating with suspense. Overall I loved this novel. A Casualty of Hope is everything readers will want and ask for in a fictional piece. Brilliantly well written and told for readers worldwide to enjoy. I highly recommend this book to all" Universal Creativity Inc14 review

"This was a riveting read that convincingly recreates a time and period in American history. The characters were well drawn and the plot skillfully developed." Amazon review

"A deftly crafted and riveting novel. A Casualty of Hope is a compelling page-turner from beginning to end. Very highly recommended." Midwest Book Review

The Girl in the Woods

Marguerite Mooers

ISBN: 978-0-9904448-1-7

Library of Congress Control Number:

LCCN Imprint Name: Potsdam, New York

To Dick, without whose help I could not make this journey

Chapter One

July 15, Day One in the Woods

The minute I got to the trailhead parking lot, my phone rang. Pulling it toward me, I guided the car to a stop and glanced at the number. It was Scott, the man I'd come to the Adirondacks to get away from.

I let it go to voicemail, and I should have put the phone away, but I listened to the message.

"Drew, it's me. Listen, Babe, I know you are pretty unhappy with me right now but I was wondering..."

In the background I could hear a baby wailing.

"Marcia, could you quiet him down," Scott yelled. And then, his voice lowered to a whisper, he said, "Drew, I never had a chance to explain all of this to you. It's not like Marcia and I planned to have a kid. I miss you, Drew. Can I come up there so we can talk?"

The kid was still wailing in the background, and I imagined Scott's life was a little bit different from when he'd been cheating on his wife with me. The message ended. It would be better for all concerned if I just let this wash over me, but I couldn't let this bozo think he could whistle and I'd come running.

I picked up the phone and dialed his number. It went to voicemail. which was probably a good thing.

"Scott, this is Drew. I'm the one you said you loved and if I would just be patient until you divorced your wife, the one you were going to marry. Only you were still sleeping with your wife, weren't you? Listen to me Scott. I am not your Babe and I am never going to see you again, talk to you again and definitely not sleep with you again. Don't call me, text me, e-mail me or try to contact me again. Ever."

I hung up the phone and tossed it into my purse, which I then locked in the trunk of my car. I hoisted my pack onto my back, with its supplies: drawing pencils, with a knife to sharpen them, paper, two granola bars and some water. I put in my camera because sometimes I will paint from photos I've taken. I was wearing shorts, a T-shirt, hiking boots, and a wide-brimmed hat. Everything else: money, phone, and sun glasses, I left in the car. I set off onto the trail, determined to paint and find my equilibrium.

When I had gone in the woods that summer afternoon, I had not planned to die.

The trail, which I'd hiked before, was lined with Beech and Hemlock, with Spring Beauties and Lady Slippers here and there on either side of the trail. Normally I would have taken my dog Lilliput along, but Lilli doesn't like the leash, especially when we're in the woods, and wrestling her down the path and keeping her out of trouble while I paint is more than I wanted to deal with.

When I'd left the apartment this afternoon, Lilli knew where I was going and resented me for it. My backpack was on the floor, and my sitting on the couch putting on my hiking boots told her that I was going hiking. "Mrs. Steen will come and walk and feed you," I said, giving her a pat. She wasn't having any of it. She followed me to the door, planting herself squarely in front of it, as if to say "You're not going without me," but I was determined.

2

Now I was in the woods, one of my favorite places in the whole world.

It is strange about my attraction to the woods. I was born and bred in New York City, where I lived until six months ago, when I moved here to Saranac Lake. The woods suited me. I liked the quiet. I liked the coolness. I liked being able to walk in silence. And, of course, now that I was trying to make my living as an artist, the woods gave me things to paint.

I had been hiking for about forty-five minutes when I realized that I'd forgotten to sign the trail register. It didn't matter. I would be out in a couple of hours and no one would be the wiser. The air, which had been cool when I started out, got gradually more sticky and oppressive as though every bit of breeze had been sucked away. By the time I'd been hiking for two hours, I was gulping water and mopping the sweat from my forehead. I was glad I'd worn a T-shirt and shorts. Maybe when I got to Beaver Lake, I would take a brief swim and then lie on a convenient rock to cool down, but in the meantime I shifted my backpack wondering if I'd brought enough water for my brief hike.

Suddenly the bright day began to darken. I looked up, through the trees, expecting rain but seeing only a glowering sky. Then the wind came up, growing stronger and stronger. Leaves and branches were flying around, and I was suddenly in a war zone with dirt and debris filling the air. Something cracked. A tree was falling, ready to hit, when I sprang away, searching frantically for shelter. Ahead of me was a boulder with a hole at the base, I rushed toward it, shoved my body into it, drawing my knees up to my chin and making myself as small as I could. The smell of pine and cut- wood drifted over me, and the wind roared above me like a freight train. A tree fell with a thwack and the ground shook, followed by a rain of leaves and branches. I pushed my face into the backpack on my knees and prayed.

And then, as suddenly as it had started, the wind died. It was deadly quiet, as though every living thing had been wiped off the face of the earth. I opened my eyes. Directly in front of me on a pile of small braches was a chickadee lying on its back, its wings fluttering weakly. I reached over and touched the bird, feeling the softness of its feathers, and seeing it grow still. Cautiously I unfolded myself and squeezed out of my hole, finding myself in a world, utterly changed. What had been forest was now open sky. All around me was a mass of jumbled trees, some lying sideways their roots still intact, others leveled at the base as though someone had taken a scythe to their trunks. The trail I'd been following was gone, the trail markers now buried under pick-up-sticks. I looked around, spotting some standing forest at the edge of the mess. Hopefully, in that intact forest, there would be another trail that I could follow back to my car. But to get there, I had to climb laboriously over one downed tree and under or around another. Having no other choice, I started toward the standing woods.

Climbing over a downed tree is hard work. It was hot and sticky and the broken limbs scratched at my naked legs. Sometimes my backpack would catch on something, pulling me up short and I would have to retrace my steps to untangle it. And this process of climbing up and over, or down and under had to be done dozens of times, so by the time I reached the standing wood, I was scratched, dirty, sweaty and exhausted. By now, it was almost five-thirty. I had promised Mrs. Steen I would be back by five, but there was no way I could do that.

I came out of the blowdown area, to find a herd path before me. This beaten-down section made by animals or hikers taking a short cut seemed promising, and I hoped I was going in the right direction. It was July, so there was still plenty of light to negotiate the way, but I worried about Lilli and how she was faring. I came to a junction, but there were no markers. Which way? I chose to go right, but after I'd gone just a little way, the trail petered out altogether. It simply was no more. I retraced my steps and took the left hand turn. I could have gone back the way I came but I knew there were downed trees blocking the path. A tiny frisson of worry bubbled up inside me. What if I were truly lost?

"I'm not lost," I said aloud. "I've been in these woods before and I know there is a trail. I just have to find it."

'What if there isn't a trail?' an inner voice asked. 'What if you can't get out?'

Today was Sunday, a day when, even in July, fewer people were hiking. I was temporarily lost, but I wasn't *really* lost. I was going to find my way home.

I continued to hike, searching the tree trunks for the metal trail markers, but there was nothing. The trail was beaten down, but was not maintained, which meant that what I was walking on might not lead me to anything. I came to another junction. Again there was no sign, but because I'd taken a left before, I took a right. I didn't want to find myself going around in circles.

I thought of Lilli at home, waiting for me, and getting frantic because I wasn't there. "Hang on sweetie," I said aloud, hoping she would somehow get the message.

I passed a place where lots of trees had fallen, which meant that I was still on the edge of the area hit by the microburst. I stopped to study the site when a bright orange cloth wedged under a downed tree caught my eye. Had someone who was camping here been caught by the storm?

Cautiously I made my way toward the entrance to the tent, climbing over the tree that had crushed it. It was possible no one was inside, which would be a good thing. I hoped that was true. Branches from the tree that had fallen on the tent were obscuring the entrance. Breaking off some branches and pushing aside others, I finally got to the entrance and was able to peer in. There, lying on his back was a young man. The bulk of the tree had landed on his chest, but his face was unmarked. His eyes were open. His mouth was open. The arm closest to me was stretched toward the entrance as if reaching for help. It was hard to see anything else inside the tent because of the bulk of the tree. I moved closer to see if he was alive. He was not.

"Shit," I said. He seemed so young. He'd probably hiked in here earlier, had decided to lie down for a nap and before he'd been able to move, the tree had killed him. When I got back to my car later, I would contact the local police to tell them about the death. I took out my sketch pad and wrote a brief note, giving my name and telephone number and saying that I hadn't touched the body. I tucked the note beside the man's head. It was hard to see anything else inside the tent but if I were reporting this death to the police I might need a picture. I took my camera and snapped a shot and, in the light from the flash, I saw a backpack. A backpack meant food, and if I were going to hike out tonight, it would be nice to have something other than the two granola bars I'd already consumed. Reaching carefully into the tent, I snagged a strap of the backpack and pulled it toward me. The backpack was heavier than my own, so I unzipped it, shoved my own smaller pack inside and then zipping it up, put it on.

It was now close to seven and getting dark. If I were going to negotiate the trail back to my car, I needed to hustle while I still had some light. Climbing back over the downed tree, I returned to the edge of the trail and taking out a bandana I tied it to a branch marking the entrance to the dead man's tent. Then I moved on.

Even though it was darker and harder to see, I moved faster hoping to reach the parking lot before full dark came on. The trail wound around, more like something created by animals than humans, but it seemed to be well packed down. Suddenly, I came to a junction. Right or left? I turned right, but in a few yards the trail simply ended. I turned left. The trail wound around for a little bit longer and then ended. Where was I? I had found myself in the situation I dreaded most. I was lost.

If you took an ordinary human being and rummaged around in their psyche you would probably find something they are deeply afraid of. Maybe it's dogs, or snakes, or speaking in public. Maybe it's visiting the doctor or being plunged into water where you can't swim. It could be simply a congenital shyness that freezes you where you stand.

I remember attending a one-woman show that my friend was having in New York City, something I envied with all the power in my little green eyes. But while people were moving around the gallery admiring the paintings, my friend was in the ladies' room, panicked.

"LeeAnne" I said, through the door to the toilet stall. "Do you know that I would give my painting hand to have this kind of show? These people are your fans, your public. This is the kind of thing an artist lives for."

"I can't do it," she said. I could hear the clink of bottle against glass as she poured herself another drink.

"You don't have to say anything, LeeAnne. Just smile and let them do the talking."

"Will you stand there with me?"

"Sure," I said. I wanted to say that she needed to suck it up and get on with it. I wanted to say that all this would pass. But I didn't mention any of those things. I couldn't say them because I had a terror of my own that was just as strong. I had a fear of getting lost.

When I was in high school, a friend invited me to her family's beach house. I decided to go for a morning walk alone, and it was only when I turned to head back that I realized I had no idea where it was. Two hours after I'd set out, I found my way back and when I told my friends what had happened, they laughed. Why hadn't I paid attention when I stepped onto the beach? Who, but an idiot like me could get so terribly lost?

These days I use my GPS when I drive to a new place, backed up with a map. When Lilli and I walk at night, it is always the same route, done from the same starting point. I am not taking any chances that I will end up on the wrong street or the wrong neighborhood, just because I'd not paid attention.

And now my deepest fear had come true. I'd been smart. I'd been careful. I'd taken a marked trail into an area of woods that I had hiked often. But I'd not brought a map, or a compass, or a flashlight to show me the way when it became dark. In spite of everything I'd done right I was now in a situation that I feared most. I was lost, and no amount of wiggling was going to get me out.

It was now almost full dark. I was not going to find my way to the parking lot tonight, and I was going to have to sleep here, in the woods. Resigned, I sat on the ground, opened the dead man's backpack, and emptied the contents on the ground. There was an almost full bottle of water, a headlamp, a sweatshirt and sweatpants, three cans of food: chicken, peas and peaches and a bag of freeze-dried pasta. At the bottom of the pack was a whistle, a Hershey bar and a copy of *Oliver Twist*.

I looked at the stuff on the ground and then shrugged myself into the sweatpants and sweatshirt, grateful for their warmth in the growing cold. I put on the head lamp, which thankfully seemed to have some battery life. This guy hadn't carried much into the woods. Maybe he was only planning to be here for a day, or maybe he had a stash somewhere else. Certainly he had a sleeping bag and pad, but the thought of negotiating my way back to the tent and poking around the body of a dead guy was way too creepy even for me. I would have to make do with what I had before me. I picked up the can of peaches and pulled open the top. Then I broke off a piece of the chocolate bar and put it into my mouth, letting it melt slowly while I slurped down the peaches. The combination was delicious, reminding me of some exotic dessert, but it wasn't much of a supper. I took a sip of water and I picked up the book. Who in the heck took *Oliver Twist* into the woods? If I were going to read myself to sleep in a tent, I would take something more exciting. I opened the book and read the first page. On the other hand, *Oliver Twist* might be just the thing to put me to sleep.

Sleeping in a tent gives you the illusion of security, even though what separates you from the outside is just thin fabric. I had nothing to protect me from the woods around me, nothing but my own brain to keep me safe. Reaching into my backpack, I found the jackknife I use to trim pencils and began cutting small pine branches. Not far from me was a rock with an overhang. I put the branches down beneath the overhang and crawled in. The branches were scratchy and sticky with pitch, but it was better than sleeping on the damp ground. I lay down on my bed of boughs, listening to the forest. Birds called to each other and then gradually grew quiet. An owl hooted and nearby something rustled; I shrugged closer to the rock at my back. I thought of Lilli alone and hungry and wondered whether Mrs. Steen, my landlady would realize that Lilly was alone and feed her. There was nothing I could do about it. What was happening was beyond my control. I am not a person who gives up easily. My last thought, before finally falling asleep, was that tomorrow I would find my way out of the woods.

Chapter Two

Day Two in the Woods

I woke early to birdsong. Sitting up, I looked through the pack for more treasures. Most of my own water was gone, but there was plenty in the other container. I opened the can of peas and slurped them down and then thought of the chocolate bar. I would have a single tiny square and save the rest for later. Chocolate. One square. I broke it off and put it on my tongue and let it melt there, remembering all the chocolaty things I love. Chocolate Mousse with whipped cream on top and raspberry syrup on the bottom, chocolate brownies, gooey and warm, chocolate chip cookies where the chips melt on your hands. Hershey's kisses, M & M's, Easter bunnies made of chocolate with frosting faces. In no time the chocolate square was gone and I realized that I needed to get myself up and walking. I stood up, fished my camera out of the pack, and snapped a picture of my sleeping spot. Maybe I would use the photo to paint a memento of spending the night in the woods.

My destination yesterday had been Beaver Lake and if I could get there, I could refill my water bottle, and because lots of people visited the lake, I might find a trail to a parking lot. I began walking, back in the direction I thought I had come from. The day was getting warmer and very soon I'd pulled off the sweat shirt and sweat pants and pulled my sun hat low over my head. I came to the fork in the road and took the path that I thought would take me past the dead man's tent. Maybe, if I went farther, I would find a place where the regular trail veered off.

It wasn't long before I found my bandana tied to the tree. I moved into the clearing, negotiating the downed tree to peer into the tent. Everything was just as I had left it the day before, except that now black ants were crawling over the man's eyes and mouth. The man was lying on a pad, which would have been nicer to sleep on than sticky branches, but did I really want to wrestle a dead man's pad out from under him? I shone the head lamp into the tent, noticing that some animal had been tossing things around, but seeing no sign of a sleeping bag, I gave up.

When you are lost in the woods how do you keep from thinking that no one is looking for you, and that you will walk around and around in this endless maze of trails that go nowhere and that someday---months or years from now, when people have stopped looking for you, a hiker will find your desiccated body in the place where you finally succumbed to the woods and died?

My solution was to sing. I sang all the Christmas carols I remembered, *Silent Night*, *God Rest Ye Merry Gentlemen*, *Deck the Halls*. I sang all the Beatles songs I remembered, *Long Day's Night*, *Hey Jude*, *Here Comes the Sun*, *I Want to Hold Your Hand*, and *Yesterday*. I sang loudly accompanying myself with an air guitar. When I'd gone through my repertoire, I tried other songs, belting out even the ones where I couldn't remember the words.

I reached another junction and tried to remember which way I'd come. There was nothing I could use as a landmark, the woods around me being uniformly the same. If I could get some perspective from higher up, I might catch a glimpse of Beaver Lake, or the parking lot or even something that looked like a trail. I turned left, looking for a candidate. There were no large rocks, but there was a tall tree that seemed climbable.

I was probably crazy to try and climb a tree. I might be a person congenitally unable to find my way back to civilization from a walk on the beach, but I was determined that I would not die in the woods.

I slung off the backpack and put it at the base of the tree. Then I grabbed a low-hanging branch and began to pull myself up. It wasn't bad going; the tree seemed willing to hold me and though I was a little weakened by a lack of food, I could find enough hand and foot-holds to hoist myself up. Soon I was near the top and though the branches were thinner, they held. Looking out I could see the area of downed trees clearly, stretching for miles. I turned and looked in the other direction and there, just at the edge was a gleam of silver. Beaver Lake? That seemed to be it.

I maneuvered my way toward the view hoping to see it better and at that moment the branch beneath my feet gave way. I grabbed a branch above me, but even as I moved toward firmer footing, the branch I was holding on to snapped and I fell.

I woke on the ground, my head pressed against a rock. Gingerly I put my hand to my head and felt a hard lump and wetness. My leg hurt and I looked down to find a large gash where I must have caught it against a broken branch. I tried to sit up, but the world was spinning and my stomach roiled. I lay back down, trying to let things settle and tried again. This time was better, but I was still dizzy, and when I finally was able to sit, my stomach rebelled and I vomited into the leaves at my feet.

I looked at my leg. The wound was not deep, but the cut was long, and I could see a bruise forming near my ankle. I took out my water bottle and poured some precious water onto the wound, trying to clean it out. Then I took the bandana from my neck and wrapped it around the leg. Even with this attention, the leg hurt like hell, and it was hard even trying to get to my feet. Reaching down, I grabbed a broken branch and getting first to my knees and then slowly, painfully to my feet, with the branch as a crutch, I began to move along. My head hurt, and the world seemed only half in focus. I had to stop often to catch my breath, to give my sore leg and aching ankle a rest and to let my stomach settle. The day was growing hotter and though I still had almost a full bottle of water, I needed to conserve it. I had read somewhere that humans can survive for up to three weeks without food, but only for three days without water. How could I fight an infection in a cut leg without water? I needed to find Beaver Lake.

I vaguely remembered seeing water from the top of the tree, but now I couldn't remember in which direction I'd seen it. I had no compass (bad mistake), no map (worse mistake), no cell phone (not bad because there is usually no cell service in these woods), and because I'd left my phone in the car, no GPS. All I had was some water, a bit of food and my own wits. I sat down on a rock, stretching my leg to give it some relief, and opened the back pack. I still had the freeze- dried food and the can of chicken, but I had no matches to start a fire, no pot to cook in, and no tool to open a can. I probably should have been brave enough to go back into the tent with a dead man and search for things I needed, but now it was too late.

I looked at the can. I might be able to smash it open with something and pour the chicken and its liquid into the dried food. After searching for a while, I found a rock, and putting the can in a flat spot I smashed down on it. The can deformed, but did not open. I smashed down again. A tiny part of the lid popped open. With my jackknife I pried open the rest of the lid and then scooping out the chicken with the same knife, I poured it into the dried food pouch.

It wasn't a great meal. The freeze-dried noodles were crunchy and the chicken was cold and greasy, which made my unhappy stomach roil in protest. But it was food and if I were going to survive, food was what I needed. After the meal, I took a drink of water, and ate two squares of the chocolate just to take the taste of the greasy chicken out of my mouth.

I stood up, thinking that if people were out looking for me, they needed to see where I was, which meant I needed to be out in the open. Just at that moment, as if on command, a helicopter buzzed overhead. My heart lifted. I hollered and waved, but of course I was deep in the woods, hidden by the trees. I reached into the pack and found the whistle and blew it loudly, but by then the helicopter had moved on.

I walked for most of the rest of the day. Once I stopped to take a picture of a tree which had been worked over by a Pileated woodpecker. If I were indeed going around in circles, this could be a landmark.

Afternoon was moving slowly toward evening, and I was still on an unmarked trail, following a herd path through cedar so dense it was like walking between walls. And then it started to rain and as the temperature plummeted, the rain turned to snow. I had no protection against the snow, only the sweatshirt and sweatpants I'd stolen from the dead man. I was tired and mercilessly hungry, and it seemed like a really stupid idea to hike in the wet. So when I found a cedar tree whose branches hung almost to the ground, I crawled underneath, and tucking my body under the branches, fell asleep.

I dreamed I was in the middle of a strange city, and my car, the only way I was going to get home, was in a parking lot somewhere. But where? In the dream it had started to snow, and I kept walking around, peering between buildings looking for the place where I'd left my car. Sometimes I would stop strangers to ask, but no-one knew where my car was. I was lost.

Chapter Three

Day Three in the Woods

I woke with a start. It was early morning and cool. Not just cool, but cold. Ice feathered the edge of the tree and when I emerged the ground was crisped and white. It was July, but weather in the Adirondacks can be freaky. To make things worse, while I'd slept some animal had gotten into my backpack, and the only food I'd had left--- my precious chocolate bar---was gone. I had nothing but water to fill my belly.

I peeled away the bandana from my wound to see how it was doing. It was swollen, there was a pink area around the cut, and it was tender to the touch. The bruise near the cut had turned a dark purple, and I was covered with bug bites. I patted some water onto the cut and re-wrapped it. Then clumsily I got to my feet, supported by my 'crutch.' If I were going to get out of here, I needed to walk.

It was harder walking today because my leg was hurting more, and I was desperately hungry. I took periodic sips of water, trying to feel less hungry, but mindful that the only water I had was what I was carrying. Black clouds were rolling across the sky and a chilly rain began to fall. I had nothing to keep the sweatshirt and sweatpants from soaking through and soon I was shivering with cold. I was still deep in the woods, where no one would find me, but the trail seemed to be rising, so I must be on a small mountain. I came to a juncture but there were no signs to guide me. Turning right I found myself on a small overlook, not very high but elevated enough to look out on the valley. There below me was water. It might be Beaver Lake, the place I'd been looking for, or it might be something else, but to get to it, I would have to negotiate a steep rocky path through thick brush. I could lie on the outcrop and hope that the helicopter I'd seen earlier would find me. Or, I could try and make my way down to the water, and now that I looked more closely, the road beside it.

I chose the walk. The rocky outcropping sloped down toward the view and was slick with ice. Cautiously I got on my hands and knees and moved toward the edge, dropping carefully down into a tangled nest of thick bushes. Luckily I had on the sweatpants, but the bushes were wet from the snow and in a very short time I was soaked. I kept going, working my way carefully down through the bushes, sometimes with no idea where my feet were planted. Once I slipped and banged my hurt leg hard. Once the backpack caught on a branch and I had to retrace my steps to unhook it. It took me most of the day to make my way down the side of the small mountain, and when I got to what I thought was the bottom, I was in thick brush. Where was the water? Where was the road? I had no idea.

I sat on a log, determined not to give in to despair. OK, I was lost. OK, it was probable that no one was looking for me. OK it was possible that even if people were looking, they wouldn't find me before I starved to death or died of hypothermia. But I had things to live for: a dog, a not-so-great job, my art, a man whom I'd loved and then run away from. Not a great list, but enough. I began to think casually about my memorial service. My mother, living in California, would come. We didn't talk often, but she was still my mother. My landlady, Mrs.Steen, and my boss, Mary Ellen Canson would most likely be there. Would Scott, the married lover I'd fled from, mourn my loss? Probably not. He was too busy with that new baby.

That was it. The list of people who would be sorry I was dead wasn't even enough for a party at a bar. How could I have lived to the age of thirty-two and have so few people care if I were alive or dead? It was a sad thought.

I could sit here and plan my funeral, I thought. That would certainly cheer me up. No, the only thing that would get me to the pond, and ultimately get me home was to get up and get moving.

I pushed through the thick bushes and found myself in blowdown. Again? Had I gone in a big circle, starting where the storm had trapped me and ending up only a little farther away? I suddenly heard a helicopter overhead and scrambling to the top of a boulder, I ripped the bandana off my leg and waived it frantically. My whistle was somewhere deep in the pack, and I had no time to find it. I waved and waved, trying to make myself visible, but the helicopter turned and flew away.

That night I slept again in the woods. My hunger had receded to a dull ache and I had the feeling of being slightly adrift in the world. Is this what dying felt like---losing your hold on everything around you and starting to float? In the middle of the night, I heard a noise and woke to find a deer, less than ten yards from me, calmly nibbling at a bit of vegetation. I knew I shared this space with other living creatures, the chickadee who'd been killed by the storm and the sneaky culprit who'd stolen my candy bar, but this was the first animal I'd seen up close. I was fixated by the grace of the deer moving through the woods, when a light at the edge of the trees caught my eye. It was pale and indistinct, almost invisible in the darkness. My heart beat faster. Maybe someone had come looking for me. Cautiously I got to my feet.

"Hello?" I called.

The light moved toward me and resolved itself into the figure of a girl. She was wearing a T-shirt and jeans and had long hair. She was like fog in the woods, a figure of light but no substance, moving through the trees. And then I realized it was a ghost.

"Carley?" I asked.

I have heard that when you are dying, you're often visited by a relative or friend who guides you on. Was this the ghost of the sister I had lost? But as the girl moved closer, I realized that though she was about the same age as my sister, it wasn't Carley. I stood up and moved toward the image. "Who are you?" I asked.

The ghost looked at me sadly, then turned and faded away. She was probably no more than a figment of my protein-starved brain, a product of hard walking, an injured leg, starvation and little sleep. I'm not a person who sees ghosts, and I don't even really believe in the afterlife, so if this spirit was out to impart some wisdom, she was telling it to the wrong person.

I lay back down and eventually, I fell asleep. I dreamed that I was riding a train. No one on the train seemed to know where we were going, but everyone seemed happy to look at the sunlit fields and shining lakes outside, content to be just where they were. As I was watching the scenery, a young woman came and sat down beside me. "This is important," she whispered. "You have to find her."

"Find who?" I asked.

"Just find her," the young woman said.

Chapter Four

Day Four in the Woods

I woke to the day coming on slowly and softly, but when I tried to rise, I was so weak that it took me several tries before I could even get to a sitting position. I reminded myself that I must be close to Beaver Lake where there would certainly be campers who would help me get home. I couldn't just give up and die here in the woods.

Slowly, painfully, I got to my knees and then to my feet. I took a sip of water from my almost empty water bottle, fished my camera out of my pack and snapped a picture. Someday, I would write an account of this. But first I had to survive long enough to get out. As I got to my knees and then was struggling to my feet, I noticed something at the edge of the trail. It was a sneaker, a woman's, size seven or eight. I hadn't seen it before I went to sleep, but it was here now. The sneaker was still clean, so it could not have been here long. Opening the backpack I tucked the sneaker inside, and then getting to my feet, I started walking.

This was a regular path, with once in a while a tantalizing, rusty trail-marker grown into the tree. Then I heard water and within a short time I was beside a little brook. Water. I could fill my bottle, which might give me more time. My last meal, which I'd eaten two days before, had been the chicken and freeze-dried noodle concoction, and now my body was starting to consume itself. Though I was determined, my muscles were weak. I didn't want to look at the wound on my leg, which had started bleeding after my fall on the hillside, because thinking about infection and blood poisoning would plunge me into despair. I needed hope. I started to sing.

It took me a long time to move a very short distance. When I'd started this morning it was barely daylight and by the time I decided to stop, judging from the sun overhead, it was almost noon. I was following the stream as it wound through the woods, but sometimes that was hard going because the rocks lining the bottom of the stream were slippery and the bank was steep and not much dryer. Twice I fell into the water, drenching my sweatpants from ankle to thigh and wetting my socks and shoes. But I kept telling myself that streams can connect to ponds and being near water meant that I could drink, and if I were going in the right direction, I might eventually find my way home.

At noon I filled my water bottle and took a long drink. Then I took off the sweatpants and the bandana and bathed my injured leg in the water. The wound looked swollen and infected and I wondered if I my leg might eventually have to be amputated.

"Stop it," I said to myself. "You are going to be rescued. It's only a matter of time."

I stood up, got my stick for support and set out again, tracing the path of the stream.

By evening, I had gone as far as my energy would take me. I found a spot not far from the water, and not even bothering to make a nest of pine boughs, I lay down on the ground. I slept without dreaming, woke to find it was bright daylight and slept again. I didn't seem to have the energy to move anymore, and even the taskmaster that had been urging me on had been stilled. I tried to shake myself out of the lethargy holding me here, but it was impossible. *I need to get up and move.* I told myself. *No one will*

21

ever find me here. This is the way people die in the woods. It was no use. I lay back and slept.

As I slept, I had a dream of wolves running through the woods talking to each other as they moved. They were running side by side, the muscles under their skin rippling as they ran, their mouths moving as they talked. "She's right around here, somewhere," one wolf said. "Hershey's got the scent," said the other wolf. I could hear crashing as the wolves came through the trees. *I've never seen a wolf up close,* I thought. *At least not one who can talk.* And then there was a wet nose on my hand and someone was saying, "Thank God she's still alive. Wake her very gently."

I opened my eyes. "Drew Morgan?" the man asked.

Chapter Five

The hospital room was bright and smelled vaguely of antiseptic. I had no memory of coming out of the woods and little memory of being brought here, but I had been rescued and I was safe. It seemed like an age since I had been in a warm, clean bed. An age since I'd had real food sitting on a table beside me. There were tubes running into my arm and my leg was heavily bandaged. But I could still could see my toes, so they hadn't amputated my leg.

"How are you feeling?" a nurse asked. She was middle-aged with graying hair and a kind smile.

"Better," I said. I looked at the glass on the table and the pitcher of juice beside it. "Could I have something to drink?"

She helped prop me up and got the straw to my mouth so I could drink.

"You were very lucky," she said. "The infection was bad, but you are responding to antibiotics. You'll probably have to walk with a cane for a while, but considering all that you went through…" She looked at me. "It could have been much worse."

"Thank you," I said.

"Don't thank me. Thank the volunteers who went out looking for you, policemen, DEC officers, firemen, helicopter pilots. That microburst killed at least six people, most of them hikers and campers. It was all in the news."

"I thought I was going to die," I said.

She patted my arm. "Well," she said. "I think you're on the mend. In fact, you're very lucky the hospital is here, close to where you were found. Otherwise you'd have been airlifted to Watertown or Syracuse."

She moved toward the door. "Can I get you anything else? I can turn on the TV so you can see the news if you want, or just give you the remote. Is there someone you need to call to tell them that you are OK?"

I needed to call my mother, Mrs. Steen my landlady, and Mary Ellen Canson, my boss, but my cell phone was in the car at the trailhead.

"Did they find my car?"

She shrugged, and moved to where a phone sat nearby. It was the kind of phone where you punch in the numbers on a keypad, but when she put it within reach, I couldn't remember my landlady's phone number.

"I left my purse in the car," I said. "That's where all the numbers are."

"I'll see what I can do," she said and left the room.

I had no time to think about calling anyone because a few minutes later, the doctor appeared. He pulled up a chair and sat down beside me. He had dark hair and glasses and I put his age about mid-thirties. His nametag identified him as Dr. Larry Turner.

"How're you feeling?"

"Better," I said.

"You are doing pretty well, considering what you went through," Dr. Turner said. "When you came in, you were mildly hypothermic, undernourished and had an infected wound. You also had a knot on the side of your head, which tells me you may have suffered a mild concussion. We were worried about sepsis from the wound, but you have a terrific immune system that worked in your favor."

"I was worried I would lose my leg," I said.

He nodded. "We try to save a limb if we can."

"How did they find me?"

He shrugged. "After the microburst, a whole army of volunteers went into the woods looking for folks. They found people who were dying, those who were already dead, and some who were injured, or just badly scared. This is a small hospital, and we have been going non-stop for about a week." He leaned back in the chair and smiled. "You had at least two strokes of luck, Miss Morgan. Having a good immune system that let your body fight the infection was the first one."

"And what was the second?"

"The truth is no one knew you were missing. Normally the rangers and local police depend on a family member or a friend to tell them when someone is missing. Then they go and check the trail register at the trailhead. But no one called about you, and you didn't sign the register, so without the microburst bringing volunteers into the woods looking for victims, no one might have gone looking. And because the microburst was such a big event, rescue was started right away."

He reached forward and laid his hand on my arm. "I don't know what it feels like to survive being lost in the woods, but

people say something like that makes them re-think their lives."
He shrugged. "You have a long life ahead of you, Miss Morgan. I
hope you use it well."

He stood up and made his way toward the door, turning just
before he exited. "We surgically cleaned the wound, and with the
antibiotics, I think it is healing. I expect within a few days you
will be able to go home."

When he'd gone, I lay back against the pillows and considered
my good luck. I'd already left a job to follow my bliss to the
Adirondacks, but I didn't have any close friends whom I loved,
only my mother on the West Coast. I should call her right now,
but all the talking with the doctor had worn me out. I had just
closed my eyes when someone knocked on the door and then
opened it. It was Estelle Steen, my landlady.

"Drew," she said brightly. "They said you'd been rescued from
the woods." She came to my bedside and hugged me hard.

"Ouch," I said.

"I'm so sorry." She looked me over. "But you're OK. When the
police called, I told them you hadn't come home, but I'm not sure
they did anything about it. By the way, Lilli misses you terribly. I
knew you hadn't come back when she was barking and barking.
Finally, I went up to your apartment and opened the door. The
poor dog had peed all over the floor. She looked so embarrassed
about it. And she was obviously starving."

"What time was this?"

"Seven o'clock on the first night you were gone. I couldn't
remember when you'd said you would be back, but it was almost
dark, so I took the dog out, fed her and then went back to my own

apartment. I thought you'd be back that night. When I didn't see you the next day, I went up and fed and walked Lilli again."

"When Monday came, I called your boss and she said she hadn't seen you, and she was getting worried. That's when I called the police."

I wondered what had happened to that call. Dr. Turner said that no one knew I was lost.

Mrs. Steen pulled her chair closer to the bed. "Is there something I can do?"

"Help me get to the bathroom," I said. I pulled back the covers, exposing my heavily bandaged leg.

"What happened?"

"I fell out of a tree."

"Fell out of a tree?"

"Long story." I was battling to sit up, and Mrs. Steen reached behind me and helped me sit. With difficulty I put both feet on the floor and then struggled to put my weight on them. Mrs. Steen put her hand under my arm and helped me stand.

"Can you bring that along?" I asked pointing to the IV stand. "I'm still attached."

Somehow I got to the bathroom, where now that I was back in civilization using a toilet was the preferred method to pee. I missed my apartment. I missed my dog. I didn't miss my job, but that was the only way I was able to support myself. If I were really going to make changes to my life based on my brush with death, what would they be?

When I got back to the bed, my phone was ringing. It was my mother.

"Drew, oh my God, Drew, are you all right. Do you want me to come there? I can do it right now. When the police called me, I said to myself. Oh God, please not Drew. I have lost one daughter; I can't bear to lose two. How are you dear?"

"I'm OK, Mom," I said. "I cut my leg which became infected, but the doctors have been able to save it, and I might walk with a limp for a while, but I'll be OK."

"You were always terrible with directions, weren't you? Remember the time you and Carley decided to walk to the golf course? You were five and Carley was three. I was so angry at you, but you didn't think there was anything wrong." My mother had started to cry, and I waited while she pulled herself together.

"Drew," she said finally, "please come to California to see me? I'll be happy to pay your way. I want to put my arms around you and know that you are all right. You are the only child I have left."

"I'll think about it, Mom," I said. "By the way, how's Roger?" Roger was my mother's current boyfriend.

"He's all right. Actually, he has decided to move out for a while, give us both some space."

"Are you OK with that?"

"Not OK. I'm not OK at all. When we first got together he thought I was a princess, and there wasn't anything he wouldn't do for me. Lately, he seems to find fault with everything. The food I cook isn't to his liking; I spend too much time at the office; I've gained weight which makes me less sexy. Last week I found the receipt for a motel room in his pants' pocket, and when I confronted him about it, he said it was a business meeting. Come on. He has an office where he can hold business meetings. It feels too much like what your father used to do to me. How is he, by the way?"

"I haven't seen him since I left New York. I get the flyers for his art shows, but he doesn't call or write."

"Well, that's typical. He was only ever interested in one person---himself. And when I wasn't paying enough attention to him, he felt he could find his fun elsewhere."

"I know Mom," I said. I didn't want to get into a conversation where we trashed my father. I remember when I was twelve, huddled in an upstairs bedroom with my sister, my hands covering her ears, and tears streaming down our faces as our parents hurled accusations at each other in the kitchen below.

"You're awfully quiet, dear," my mother said.

"I was thinking about Carley," I said. "Tomorrow will be the fifteenth anniversary. She would have been thirty. And maybe have a husband and family."

"Or maybe she would have stayed single like you."

"Missing her never goes away, does it," I said. "I find myself looking at a dress and thinking, 'Carley would look great in that,' or listening to a song we both loved and remembering singing it together at the top of our lungs." I could feel the tears starting.

"Two weeks ago, I had to testify at *his* parole hearing. (We always referred to Carley's killer as 'he' or 'him', never by his real name.) The judge ruled against giving him parole, so there's no chance he will ever leave jail."

"I wish they'd given him the death sentence, Mom."

"I think life without parole is worse. It means he has the rest of his life to think about what he did." There was a long pause. " I've got to go honey. I've got a client coming in ten minutes. I'm glad we talked, and I'm delighted that you are OK. Think about a trip to California. I love you."

"Love you."

Chapter Six

The return to my normal life was strange, as though I'd been living on another planet and life on earth now had a tinge of weirdness. I appreciated sleeping in a bed again, and I ate well, trying to put back on the pounds I'd lost in the woods. And then, two days after I got out of the hospital I returned to my job at Adirondack Made. The store, standing right on Main Street, was an art gallery, gift shop and coffee shop. We did our best business in the summer when tourists swarmed through town.

"Drew," Mary Ellen, my boss said, seeing me limp with my cane into the store. She came toward me and put her arms around me. "Do you know that you and the storm are both local celebrities?"

She went behind the counter and pulled out a stack of newspapers. "I saved all of these in case you wanted to see what you missed." She put the papers on the counter, in chronological order. The headline for July 16th read "Microburst Roars Through Southern Adirondacks" above a photo of massive blowdown, just like what I'd seen up close.

"I can't believe you were right there when it happened."

"It was like being under a freight train. The trees were falling all around me," I said. "I finally found a hole in a bottom of a rock and ducked into it."

The headline for July 17th read " Volunteers, DEC and Local Police Looking for Survivors" and for July 18th "Six Dead, Eleven Injured: Campers and Hikers Evacuated."

31

For July 19th, the headline read "Local Girl Found After Four Days in Woods" Below was a grainy picture of me.

"Where did they get the picture?" I asked.

Mary Ellen pulled out a brochure. "Did you forget the town-wide art fest we had this spring? We put out a brochure advertising the artists." She handed me the brochure. The picture wasn't great, but it was definitely me.

"We sold one of your pictures too," she said.

I looked around, trying to remember what I'd hung in the small gallery.

"The one with the tree growing out of the rock."

"No doubt a pity purchase."

"I don't think so. Lots of people came in to tell me how they admired you for sticking it out until you got found. A few came in with these." She went back to the desk, pulled out four plastic compasses and dumped them into my hands. One of the compasses was actually a bright orange whistle with a small compass set into the side.

"Nice of them," I said.

"Well, you know. It's a small town. People care about each other."

Just at that moment a customer came in, and we retreated to our stations, trying to look like this hadn't been the first customer in what might be a long, un-busy day.

At noon Mary Ellen and I sat down together for lunch, eating sandwiches we had made ourselves in the backroom.

"Drew," Mary Ellen said. "I've been thinking about the store." I looked at her. When I'd been hired in the spring, she had said that she usually closed the store around the end of October. By then, the hikers, boaters, and those who rented camps in the area were gone and it made no sense to pay rent on a store that wasn't selling anything.

"Things have been slow," she said. "I've been thinking that beginning in mid-August, I'm going to go to one employee."

"One employee? You mean you." In order to find another job at this time of year, I would have to travel to Lake Placid or even Watertown. Damn.

She moved toward me to give me a hug, but I shrugged away. "I'm sorry," she said. "I know I promised I would keep you until October, but it just isn't possible."

It was now July 24th and I needed to hustle around if I were going to replace one job with another, especially when most businesses were closing for the season. So after I got off work that evening, I drove around the area asking in restaurants, motels, souvenir shops, book stores, even galleries for any job that might be available. I washed up my search at the Sleepy Inn Motel on the edge of town which was in need of a maid who would help the overworked single employee. Arlette Patchett, the owner/manager, was a rail-thin chain smoker with dyed red hair and a deep cough.

"You'll need a uniform, which we will supply but the cost will come out of your first week's wages, and there's a two week lag time between when you start work and when we issue you a check." She looked at me carefully. "You have done this sort of work before?"

"I have," I lied. She looked at the cane. "Do you always need that?"

"It's just for the next couple of days until my leg heals," I said.

Arlette showed me where the carts were kept and said my hours would be Monday through Friday eight-thirty to three-thirty. The pay was less than I'd been making at Adirondack Made, but I still had a little in savings, and it was a job. Starting a new job before my old job ended was a little bit awkward, but I don't think Mary Ellen minded. She asked if I would work Saturdays for another two weeks and I agreed. In fact, I think she was bit relieved that I had found something else.

In spite of having a new job, I was still depressed about my situation, and as I walked Lilli that evening, I considered my options. I could go back to New York and live with my father, and possibly get another job in the same field as the one I left. But being in the same city, and working for another ad agency, meant probably running into my former lover, his wife and child. If I stayed here for the winter, and didn't get laid off again, I might be able to make it.

I had returned from my walk and was heating up leftovers for supper when there was a knock on my door. It was Mrs. Steen, my landlady.

"Drew," she said from the doorway. "Can I ask you a favor?"

"Sure," I said. I motioned her in. "Would you like a glass of wine, or soda?"

"Wine? Sure," she said. She was sitting on the edge of the seat, twisting her hands together. I waited.

"There's a medium here in town on Saturday night and I want to go and see her."

What did this have to do with me?

"I want you to come with me. Moral support and all." She leaned forward in the chair. "I've been thinking about Arthur, my late husband. He's been gone for five years now, and I want to talk with him, but I can't bear to go to this medium alone. If you come with me, I'll pay your way."

I could plead that I had a date, but I hadn't had anything like that since I'd moved here in the spring, and Mrs. Steen's apartment was right below mine, so she would know if anyone came up to see me. In addition, she had been the one who'd walked and fed Lilli when I was stuck in the woods. She had been the one who'd called the Sheriff and said that I wasn't home. I owed her a lot. I could certainly spend an evening holding her hand while she visited some medium.

"Sure," I said. "What time does the thing start?"

"Eight o'clock. I'll pick you up at seven-thirty."

"Isn't that a little early?"

"I want to get a good seat. Don't you?"

Inwardly I groaned. On Saturday I would be working at the store, which meant I would have to rush home, give Lilli an abbreviated walk, and eat a hasty supper, all so I could sit in a near- empty room, while smarter people had a leisurely supper and still got a good seat. But I had said yes and couldn't back out now.

Chapter Seven

Promptly at seven-thirty on Saturday night, Mrs. Steen presented herself at my door. I wasn't looking forward to this, but I steeled myself. True to my prediction when I got to the hall, only three of the twenty seats were occupied. Mrs. Steen settled herself in a seat in the first row and we waited. Slowly the room began to fill up with what seemed to be middle-aged women. One woman congratulated Mrs. Steen on bringing her daughter as moral support. She'd tried to talk her own daughter into it and had been firmly refused.

"Of course," the woman said. "She's eighteen, and you know how teens are."

At quarter to eight, a man came into the room, stepped up to the podium, adjusted the mike and then left. Then at eight a small woman with bright red hair and huge glasses walked up to the front of the room. She was wearing a dark blue caftan embellished with silver stars. I would have guessed that she was in her forties, but with the amount of makeup she was wearing she could have been ten years older. Given the hair, the makeup and the dress, I'd have pegged her as just a showman, but when she began to speak in a low, mellow voice, I changed my mind. Maybe this wouldn't be so bad.

"Before we begin tonight, I want to tell you a little about myself," she said. "My name is Celestina. I was born into a family of Italian immigrants who were devout Roman Catholic and very strict. When I started in the fifth grade, I found that sometimes I knew who was gravely ill, even before anyone said a word. Once, during class, I told my grade school teacher that her son had tried to hang himself at home but that he'd been found just in time. She told me I was crazy and that I didn't know what I was talking about, but a few minutes later, the principal came into the classroom. I watched as they talked and the teacher burst into tears."

"The next day my teacher told me that what had happened had been exactly as I described it. I expected her to be angry with me, but she said I had a gift, and no one should be allowed to diminish it. Of course my family thought I wasn't normal, my playmates told me I was weird, and I tried not to talk about what I knew. It wasn't until I was in my twenties that I was introduced to people who could communicate with those on the other side. I knew then that I could use my gift to help others."

There was a scattering of applause. Celestina gave a small bow and then said, "You are all here to speak to your loved ones who have passed over. I want you to understand that those who have passed have free will. Much as you would like them to appear, I cannot force a spirit to do anything. I can only communicate with those who want to talk to you."

She closed her eyes and took a deep breath. Then she opened them. "Mary Evans," she said. "Is Mary here?"

A woman in the back row raised her hand shyly.

"I am seeing a man, he is big and strong looking. He's got dark hair and is wearing glasses. He says he is Ralph your husband."

Mary nodded.

"Ralph is very angry," Celestina continued. "In fact he is shouting at me right now, making it hard to hear what he's saying.

Please, let me try to get him to calm down." There was a pause. "That's better."

"I need to tell you Mary, that I only repeat what the spirit says to me. I don't put words in their mouths. Ralph wants to say that you are a bitch."

There was a collective gasp and a few titters. I looked over at Mary who had turned deep red and had her head down.

"He says he should have divorced you a long time ago, instead of hanging on the way he did. The only reason he stayed was for the children's sake. I am sorry to say this, but those are his words."

I peeked at Mary, feeling sorry for her. It's hard enough to be dissed in person, but how do you fight a ghost?

Celestina had moved to a different part of the room and had closed her eyes again. "I have a young woman who wants to speak to someone named Drew." Celestina opened her eyes. "Is Drew here?"

My mouth went dry and I looked around. No one else had raised their hand, so I put mine up.

"She says her name is Carley. Do you have a sister who passed?

I nodded, feeling the tears starting.

"Carley wants to tell you that that you are an amazing artist, and don't worry about your love life. The right man is going to come along soon."

I nodded again.

"There's someone else here. She says that you don't know her, but her name is Molly. She is telling me that you need to find the girl."

"Find the girl?"

"That's what she is telling me. It's critical. You need to find the girl as soon as you can."

Mrs. Steen leaned toward me. "Ask her about Arthur," she whispered.

Celestina turned to Mrs. Steen. "I'm sorry, Madam. As I said earlier, I can't force spirits to come when we want them." She moved away. "Helen Atkinson, are you here?"

Helen raised her hand and Celestina began relaying a message from Helen's son, who had been killed in Iraq and who wanted to tell her that he was OK, and was grateful for the flowers she was putting on his grave. Next we heard from Alice Gottlieb who'd died ten years before and told her husband, Stan that she loved him, but he needed to move on instead of sitting at home mourning her. Leanne Steiner's father said that he was watching over her and was very proud of his daughter. Arthur never showed up.

"Well, that was a waste of twenty dollars," Mrs. Stein said, as we were putting on our coats. She leaned toward me and whispered. "I think she's a fraud."

"Shhh…" I said. "She's coming over here."

When she got closer, I noticed that Celestina was not quite as young as I had originally thought. Not forties, fifties, maybe. Even sixties.

"Drew," she said, holding out her hand to shake mine. "I wanted to talk with you about Molly. She seemed very anxious that you understand her message."

I nodded.

"You were the woman who was lost in the woods, weren't you? I remember reading about it."

I nodded again.

Celestina took a deep breath. "Sometimes, very rarely, when a spirit passes suddenly, they get stuck in limbo. They don't have people on the other side who reach out to them and they don't successfully process their death, so they hang around."

"Like ghosts?"

She nodded. "I don't sense this with your sister, but I think it happened with Molly, the other young woman."

All of this was new to me. I thought when someone died, they just died.

"I remember a case I had early on. An elderly man, who was living alone had a heart attack in his basement. Instead of passing over he stayed where he was, confused and angry. The house stood empty for three years, and when new people moved in, he began haunting the house, making noises in the night, waking up a teen-age son, that sort of mischief. Finally, the family came to me. I was able to meet with the man on the astral plane and convince him that he would be happier moving on and being with friends who loved him."

Mrs. Steen was tugging at my coat. She'd clearly had enough of this.

Celestina took a card from her pocket and handed it to me. "Come and see me. I do private readings and maybe we can help Molly find her way to the afterlife."

"Why is she contacting me? I'm sure we've never met."

"It is possible that you were just close to the place where she died." She closed her fingers over the card in my hand. "Call me," she said.

All the way home, Mrs. Steen complained about Celestine's lack of professionalism, and how she'd never get suckered into paying money for any of that crap again. I hardly heard her. I was trying to understand how I might have come in contact with a girl named Molly. And then, I remembered the ghost that had appeared when I was starving and lost. Maybe this was Molly, and she was contacting me now because we'd been in the woods together, she already dead, and I close to dying.

Chapter Eight

My new job in the motel was harder than I'd expected. I could usually clean five rooms in the time allotted, but it was a full day of making beds, cleaning bathrooms, and picking up random stuff dropped by guests. Sometimes when I'd been with the ad agency, I would stay in a hotel as part of a conference, but now, after cleaning the toilet, sink, and tub, reloading the clean soap, shampoos, conditioners, mouthwash, changing the toilet paper, making beds, vacuuming the rugs, cleaning the microwave and refrigerator, and running my rag over all the surfaces, I wish I'd tipped more generously.

After a full day of work, I was ready to treat myself to supper out. The restaurant, Manny's, specialized in Italian food and looked out over Lake Flower. I was sitting at a table, with Lilli at my feet , the both of us squeezed up against the side of the patio fence. I was drinking Sangria and reading a book when we were interrupted. If you are a single woman eating alone, a book always makes it seem as though you are just there to eat and read, and you're not a single woman looking to pick up a man.

"Drew Morgan?"

I looked up to see a tall man wearing a green uniform and a park ranger's Smokey-the-Bear hat.

"Am I under arrest?"

He smiled. It was a nice smile, but even with the smile he was still a man in a uniform, with that larger-than-life, official stance that a uniform promotes.

"Can I join you?" he asked.

I nodded. He sat opposite me, took off his hat and laid it carefully on the seat beside him. He had rusty-colored, curly hair, and when he took off his sun glasses I saw his blue eyes. His tan, the shadow of a beard, and the muscles that bulged under his short-sleeved shirt convinced me that here was a man who not only spent his day outdoors, but worked out. Lilli rose and padded over to the man, putting her head on his lap. He patted her head and spoke to her quietly.

"Golden?" he asked.

"Heinz 57. She followed me home one night, and I decided to keep her."

He held out his hand to shake mine. His was long-fingered and freckled but with a strong grip. "I'm Matt Waring," he said. "I'm one of the guys who found you in the woods. I'm glad to see that you're doing well. How's the leg?"

I raised my bare leg and waggled my sneaker-clad foot, so he could see the scar. He bent down to inspect it, and his warm breath on my leg sent a frisson of excitement through my body.

"You were lucky," he said.

"So they tell me."

"Well," he said, rising. "I won't keep you from your drink. I am just glad that you're OK."

"Wait," I said. "Please stay. The least I can do is buy you a drink."

"My dog was actually the one who found you."

"Then I should buy your dog a drink."

"He's a teetotaler," Matt said.

"What breed is your dog?"

"He's a chocolate lab, named Hershey. He's in the car right now. If you don't think the two dogs would argue, I can bring him here."

"I don't mind," I said. A waiter had appeared, and Matt took a quick glance at the menu, ordered a meal and a beer and then went to get his dog. A few minutes later he had returned with a large exceptionally well-behaved chocolate lab, who settled at his feet, ignoring Lilli.

When his beer had come, I asked. "Do you spend a lot of time looking for people in the woods?"

"Much more than we used to. With more people in the woods, more folks are getting lost. People go into the woods thinking they can rely on their cell phones. They have apps for compasses and maps, even flashlights, but batteries go dead or there is no cell service. The hikers who've never been in the woods before don't think of the danger. The other day I stopped a couple going up Mt. Ampersand. She was wearing shorts and a T-shirt and flip flops. Flip flops. Can you believe it? It had rained the day before and the trail was muddy. Mud on the Adirondack trails is strong enough to pull *my* boots off, and I knew in a short while she'd be barefoot. I very forcefully suggested that she should not hike up into the mountains where she would have to negotiate roots, rocks and mud in flip-flops. "

"You didn't pull out your gun and march her back out?"

He smiled. "Can't do that. Not unless they are actually breaking the law, but sending a team up into the mountains to rescue someone is an expensive, time-consuming proposition, and the rangers are already stretched to the max. Luckily I was able to get her out with a minimum of hassle."

"So, in addition to looking for lost hikers what else do you do?"

"I try to keep people from camping illegally. If they're camping at a lean-to, I make sure they have a bear-proof canister for their food. It seems unfair to the bear to put food in easy reach, and then have to relocate that animal because it's being a nuisance. After all, the woods are the bear's home; it's only taking what's freely offered."

Our meals had arrived, and we tucked in. I could hear Lilli snoring at our feet. Out beyond the patio, darkness, like a grey blanket was being drawn across the sky, leaving only a tiny glimmer of light at the horizon. A few geese honked, and lights along the shoreline winked. I could smell food cooking in the kitchen.

"You were lucky we found you, you know," Matt said.

"Dr. Turner told me that if it hadn't been for the microburst, no one would have gone looking for me," I said.

"Especially since you didn't sign the register."

"Guilty as charged," I said.

"If you hadn't left that note with Helmut Aronson, we never would have gone looking for you."

"Helmut Aronson?"

"The dead man in the tent. Helmut's mother called as soon as the microburst hit and said her son was in the woods alone. When we found your note, we realized that there was someone else nearby we hadn't known about. We weren't sure how long you'd been in the woods and whether you'd been hurt by the storm."

"But you'd have found my car in the parking lot?"

"Possibly. And we would have matched your plates to your name. But with all the people in the woods that day, we were very busy, and we might not have realized you were out there until much later. You owe your life to a dead man."

I nodded, sobered.

I took a sip of my drink and glanced down at Hershey, who had fallen asleep. "Does Hershey ever get sad after finding a dead person in the woods?"

Matt shook his head. "I'm the one who gets depressed. I know if the dead person had gone a quarter of a mile or even a hundred yards in the right direction, he might have been rescued. That's what gives me nightmares. But for Hershey it's all part of the game. We have to treat it like that, because finding people dead or alive is hard work. Search and rescue dogs work in crumbling buildings after an earthquake, in tight spaces after an explosion, or with toxic dust like the stuff that fell from the World Trade Center. For a dog, the joy is in finding the prize and of course, getting his reward. Being rewarded and praised is what keeps him going."

He took a sip of his beer. "I'm glad to see your leg is better. How are you doing otherwise?"

"Not so well," I said. "At first it felt strange to be back among the living. When I saw how many had been injured in the microburst, I was overcome with guilt. I had survived, by sheer luck, when so many people hadn't. And then it seemed like I should do something with that luck, become something better than I was, but of course I didn't know how to do that. I went back to selling coffee and art at Adirondack Made. But that job ended a few weeks ago and now I'm making beds and cleaning toilets at the Sleepy Inn Motel near here".

"When I got back from Iraq I was rootless and unhappy. There was no one I could talk to about what I'd been through. My wife was willing to listen, but then she got tired of the same old stories, and she started to wonder when I would just snap out of it."

I hadn't missed the part about his wife. I looked down, but he wasn't wearing a ring. That didn't mean anything. Lots of married men, including the one I'd hooked up with at my previous place of employment, hadn't worn one. "You seem to have weathered it well," I said.

"The dogs brought me back. You know the saying 'he's going to the dogs?' In my case it was just the opposite. I went to the dogs and the dogs helped me get sane. A friend of mine is into training search and rescue and body dogs. Search and rescue dogs look for live victims, body dogs look for dead victims. Sometimes they are the same dog, sometimes different dogs."

"Jim Weims, my friend, was also a veteran who'd had a hard time adjusting and sort of fell into the job because he had a border collie, named WhizBang who went nuts when he was left alone. Jim said he needed something for his dog to do, and in finding a job for the dog, he found a life for himself."

Matt looked down at his plate which was still half full. I had polished mine off while he was talking. I looked around the restaurant, which had emptied out considerably since we'd come in.

"So you went with your friend who was training a dog for search and rescue."

"Yeah," that smile again, warm, inviting. Oh dear, this was way too soon. "Whiz had a good nose, which is what you want with a search and rescue dog, but he was undisciplined and made lots of mistakes. Of course Jim made lots of mistakes too. Mostly during the first year, I just stood around watching, wondering if this kind of thing could bring me back to life."

"And was it?"

"It was, eventually. It couldn't save my marriage, but being with a dog saved me. We were doing something together--- learning together. The first time we went on a real search, which was about four years after I got my dog, I began to think the job could bring me back to a sense of myself that I'd lost after the military. The case was a little boy who'd gone out on his own and got stuck in a drain pipe he crawled into. We found him that day and when I got home that night, for the first time in a long time, I felt hopeful, optimistic. I had saved a life. Five years later, after some training, I became part of the park ranger canine team."

We had finished our meal and our drinks. There seemed to be nothing else to say.

"Would you like to come out with Jim and me this Saturday and see what the dogs can do?" Matt asked. "You can bring Lilli if you want."

I nodded. I loved dogs. I had watched border collies do their stuff once at sheepdog trials and marveled at these amazing animals who could be so helpful on the field but still be loving pets.

"Give me your number and I'll call you," he said.

I rummaged through my purse and found an old receipt from a gas purchase. I wrote my number on it.

"Thanks for the beer," he said.

"Beers."

"The beers. I'm glad you're doing well, Drew."

I got up from the table and started moving away when a thought occurred to me.

"Matt," I said.

He turned. God he was good looking, but I needed to focus on the question.

"Did they find everyone who was in the woods when the microburst hit?"

His face grew serious. "We're pretty sure we did. We have only the trail registers to go by and whoever calls the DEC about a missing person. If someone walks into the woods without signing in, it is possible they are still there. God, I hope that isn't true."

"I saw someone in the woods," I began, realizing even as I said it that he would probably classify me instantly as a nut-job, someone who'd fallen on her head once too often.

"Someone?"

"A teenage girl. But I think she was a ghost."

"You saw a ghost in the woods?" I could hear the doubt in his voice.

"It was almost the last day, and maybe I was hallucinating, but I'm sure I saw her. And I found a shoe."

Now he seemed interested. "What kind of shoe?"

"A sneaker. It belonged to a woman and was fairly clean. I know people sometimes carry extra shoes on their packs, but it seemed strange that I would find a shoe right after I saw the ghost."

Matt nodded. "Those things happen," he said. He took hold of Hershey's leash, turned and was gone.

Why had I decided to tell him about the ghost? Not only was he not going to pursue the thought that there was someone dead in the woods, but I'd probably blown any chance I had to become better friends. That is if I wanted to be friends. Matt was good looking, but probably married, and even though he'd invited me to come and see his dogs work, it was most likely just professional friendliness. I felt loneliness settle down over me like a mist. I was pretty happy with the choice I'd made to drop everything in New York City and do my Adirondack-wild-woman thing here, but sometimes I missed the bustle of the city, the all night movie theatres, the ethnic restaurants. I missed my chums at the firm, and sometimes, though I hate to admit it, I missed Scott.

Matt Waring stood by his car and watched Drew walk from the restaurant to the street, her dog trotting along beside her. She had certainly changed from the wan girl they had carried out of the woods three weeks ago. Then he hadn't believed that someone as small as she was, five two and weighing a little more than a hundred pounds could survive four days in the woods with no food or shelter. When he'd first seen her, her glossy dark hair had been limp and dirty, now it shone and her eyes were full of fun. He'd seen men die in the woods after less time, men who'd gone in with guns and enough ammunition to kill for food, but who had succumbed to cold, starvation and finally despair. Something had pulled him into her orbit. How long had it been since he'd been attracted to a woman? How long had it been since he'd thought about anything other than work? They might be together this weekend, and he'd see where it went from there.

Chapter Nine

That night I dreamed that I was lost in a strange city. Lost. A lot of my dreams are about being lost. This time, I was trying to find my way to my car which I'd parked somewhere, but had no idea where. After wandering around for at least an hour, I finally went into a small grocery store. The clerk at the store was a teenager with long blonde hair and lots of makeup.

"Hi," I said, feeling foolish. "I'm looking for a parking lot in this city that is right next to a Chinese restaurant. Can you tell me where it might be?"

Instead of answering directly the girl began to cry. She was telling me something but, because she was crying, it was hard to hear her. I reached forward across the counter and took her hands in mine. "What's wrong?"

"You need to find her," she said. "You need to find the girl."

I woke to the sun streaming through the window. I got out of bed, put on a robe and walked to the kitchen for coffee. Lilli followed, looking up at me eagerly.

I picked up her food dish and began filling it. "You need to cut down on these carbs," I told the dog. "They'll go straight to your hips." The dog, impervious to my suggestions, dug into her bowl. I still had plenty of time before my job started, and we could go for a long run along the lake before I had to go to work. I was probably more in need of a strict diet than she was.

"Find the girl," the woman in my dream had said. What girl? I didn't know any girl who was lost. Had my time in the woods affected me more than I knew? I needed to talk with someone.

I picked up the phone book and began to work through the yellow pages, looking for a therapist. I'm not someone losing her mind. I had been, still am, an artist with a good brain, but something had happened to me, first in the woods and now in my dreams that needed to be resolved.

The therapist's name was Dr. Sharon Limbeck, and things must have been slow for her, because she gave me an appointment two days later. Her office was on a side street in what appeared to be a private home. I was used to big city offices, in high rises with lots of glass and modern furniture, but maybe having an office in your own home meant affordability. I rang the bell and a tall woman wearing jeans and a T-shirt answered. She had a curly hair, glasses that overwhelmed her face and a kind smile. She was wearing a stained apron.

"Sorry," she said, pulling off the apron. "I was cleaning up the garden." She led me to a small sitting room that looked out over a back yard and a garden in enthusiastic display.

"I love your garden," I said.

"My own mental health therapy," she replied, gesturing to a leather chair. "Please sit."

I sat. Dr. Limbeck took a pad of paper and a pen from the table and set them on her lap. She glanced back at the desk. "I've been trying to give up smoking," she said. "Tried all the tricks I usually advise my clients to use, but…" She sighed. "Tell me what brings you here."

I described the recent dream. I didn't tell her about the message from Madam Celestina, or the other dreams.

"You're the one who got lost in the woods after the microburst," Dr. Limbeck said. "When you called, I remembered I'd seen your name in the paper. I'm not surprised that you're having a reaction."

So much for small town anonymity. "So all of this is because I was lost in the woods?"

"Drew," she said, leaning forward. "You survived a microburst and then you wandered around, starving and with a terrible wound. I'm not surprised that you're having a reaction. My surprise would be if you had none at all."

"Wow," I said.

"Yeah. Wow. When a person lives through what you've experienced, there has to be some psychic bruising. Sometimes it's just a strong reaction, but often there is actual damage that can take years for the patient to work through. The world seems strange and different. You have trouble sleeping. The people you were close to no longer seem to have the same values. It's as though you have come home to a different world than the one you left."

"I feel guilty," I said. "Why did I survive and others didn't? And it's hard getting used to sleeping in a bed again, eating whatever I feel like, using a bathroom. The main problem is that now I have this terrible fear of going back into the woods, and I love the woods."

"Anything else?"

"Lilliput, my dog, and I used to wander all over town together when we went for a walk. Now I stick to routes that I know. It's like if I divert my path even a little I will be back in the woods, terrified, and dying and unable to save myself."

"But you have been saved. You've been given another chance. All of these things are normal reactions to what you experienced. My advice to you is to go back into the woods. Take only the paths you are very sure of, and only go for a short time. Maybe hike for a quarter of a mile and come back. The next time you go, hike for a little bit longer, a mile perhaps. Build up your tolerance for the woods little by little, and I think you will eventually overcome your fear. It will take time, but I think you are going to heal."

"Anything else?"

"This will take time. Don't expect it to happen overnight." She looked down at the pad on her lap. "Do you take a backpack into the woods?"

"Sure," I said.

"What I suggest is that you set up an emergency backpack with a map, a compass, some way to make a fire in the woods, a Mylar blanket, and a brightly colored piece of cloth to signal with. The next time you go into the woods take the backpack with you. What happened to you will probably never ever happen again, but this time you'll be prepared." She looked at her watch. Our session was almost over. She reached forward and grasped my hand, and when I rose, she gave me a hug. It was only after I'd left that I remembered that I'd never mentioned the ghost.

Chapter Ten

I was sitting on my aged sofa in my old sweats with Lilli's head on my lap and an old sitcom on TV when the phone rang.

"Hello?"

"Drew?"

"Scott," I said. *Damn, I should have checked the number before picking it up.*

"I'm just phoning to see if you're OK."

"I'm OK," I said. "Scott, I told you not to call me."

"I came across a copy of an Adirondack newspaper that said you'd almost died in the woods. I called because I was concerned."

"I'm OK, Scott. How's the baby?"

"He's fine. To tell you the truth, I'd forgotten how much work new babies are."

"Puts a big kink in your sex life, I'll bet."

"I thought you'd be happy to hear from me. I was concerned about you. We had something nice going, didn't we?"

"Did you think that we were just going to pick up where we left off? Sneaking off at lunchtime for a quickie, but never being able to have a nice meal in public or even have you meet my friends? I've smartened up, Scott. Don't call me again." I hung up, proud of myself for telling him off, but also desperately longing for him. I remembered the scent of his aftershave, the way he could give me goose bumps just touching my arm. I thought about his dark eyes and the hair falling over his forehead which I always wanted to brush away. How could I ever have fallen for him? But I had.

I reached for the remote and flipped on the TV again, going to Netflix and surfing through the offerings. I had just started watching a movie when the phone rang again.

"Hello?"

"Drew? It's Matt. Would you still like to come out with us this weekend? You were interested in what S & R dogs do. This will be your chance."

"Sure," I said. "You said Lilli would be invited."

"Of course, we'll just be working the dogs, and then we might go for lunch. I'll pick you up at your place. Give me your address."

I told him.

"Nine o'clock? Before it gets too hot. And dress in something you don't mind getting dirty."

"Thanks," I said.

"You're welcome. It will be nice to have you there."

I couldn't read too much into that last sentence. He was going to show me how the search and rescue dogs practiced, that was all. I looked down at Lilli who'd fallen asleep with her head on my lap. "Lil," I said, moving her head. She opened her eyes and looked at me. "You've got a date on Saturday," I said. "With a good looking guy named Hershey."

Marguerite Mooers

She closed her eyes, unimpressed, and began to snore.

Chapter Eleven

At eight forty-five Lilli and I were waiting at the front door to the apartment building. I'd dressed in old jeans and a long sleeved shirt, and I'd stuffed granola bars, three large bottles of water, dog food, Lilli's food bowl, a sun hat and bandana into a backpack. I'd also put in a T-shirt and shorts to change into later. It was August, and even at eight forty-five, I could feel the heat starting to rise. Hopefully we would be in a place where we wouldn't bake in the sun.

I watched as a Land Rover turned down the driveway and pulled up in front of me. Matt hopped out and opened the door to the back. A metal crate with Hershey inside filled most of the space. "You've met my dog before," he said. He looked at Lilli. "Does she have a crate?"

"She never goes anywhere," I said. "In fact this is the first time she's been with a guy in ages. She's very excited, but she'll behave."

"OK," he said. He put Lilli's front paws on the back of the vehicle and lifted her hindquarters. An old quilt had been thrown into the space between the crate and the wall and she settled down. Hershey put his head next to the bars and took a good sniff, but Lilli turned away. Since they'd already met, they were going to behave.

Matt slammed the door, and I hurried around to the side, opening the door and climbing in before he could do the polite-guy thing and open the door for me. When we were on the road,

Matt said, "Jim's going to be there. I told you about him right? WhizBang was Hershey's mentor, but Whiz is thirteen now and too old to go out on search and rescues. You know how it is, when your mind knows what to do, but your body can't do it any more? Sometimes I watch Whiz when Hershey is working and I can almost hear Whiz still trying to give him pointers. Each dog has a different way of working, a different way of signaling that he's found something. Whiz is an exuberant personality. When he finds the victim, he drops down to the ground and howls or barks. There is no way you can miss his signals. Hershey will stay in one place and point, or if you aren't paying attention he'll come over and almost drag you to the spot."

I thought about Lilli. It would be interesting to see if she had any inclination toward search and rescue.

As if reading my mind, Matt said. "The first thing we'll do this morning is test Lilli's nose. You're still interested in training her?"

"Is it a lot of work?"

"A lot, but it's fun. At least the dogs think so."

We were out of town now, moving into the countryside, heading toward Tupper Lake. On either side of us were forests, giving way occasionally to the edge of a pond with distant views of the mountains. We slowed, then turned up a driveway to a parking lot beside a large, grey two- story cement-block building that had once been a factory. Part of the building was still standing, but part had been knocked down, so it was now partly a pile of cement blocks tossed haphazardly. Grass was pushing up through the pavement of the lot, and woods had encroached on what might have been fields. I could see piles of logs partly hidden by small trees that had grown up around them.

"This was a paper mill, before paper mills left the area. We got the fire department to help us knock down part of it, so we could replicate a building that the dogs might encounter after a fire, tornado or earthquake." Beyond the knocked-down building were open woods where I could see blue barrels set on their side.

"What are those?"

"Training places. We take turns hiding in the space, and the dogs practice finding us."

At that moment a SUV pulled up, and a tall man with salt and pepper hair got out. Matt got out of the car and slapped the other man on the back. I got out too.

"This is Drew," Matt said. "She's going to work with us today. Jim Weims."

"You're interested in having a search and rescue dog?" Jim asked.

"I don't know," I said. "To tell you the truth until I met Matt, I hadn't thought about it."

"It's not a job for everyone." Jim said, moving to the back of the SUV and opening the door. I could see a medium sized border collie in a crate.

"Was your dog one of the ones who rescued me?"

"He was part of the team, yeah. Unfortunately, WhizBang is getting too old for this stuff. Arthritis in the hips. But he loves this work and he's good at it. When I'm going out on a search without him, he gets very depressed. Come on," he said. "Let's give these guys some air."

Jim released the latch on a crate and lifted the dog to the ground. Matt had released Hershey from his crate, and Lilli had climbed down on her own. The three dogs walked around each other, sniffing butts and generally getting to know each other.

"She's neutered, right?" Jim asked me.

I nodded.

"How old is she?"

"Three, I think. I found her as a stray, and she'd obviously been on the street for a while because she was thin and scabby."

Jim was watching the dog. "She seems to have a good temperament, and she might not be too old. It takes a while to train a dog, so you want to start as young as possible. Do you want to test her?"

"I don't want to keep you from what you're going to do today," I said.

He shrugged. "We have plenty of time. Let's do the easy stuff first---make it fun for the dogs."

He went back to the car and came out with three small buckets with mesh bottoms. Turning them upside down, he lined them up in a row.".

"We'll do this one dog at a time," he said. He took a treat from his pocket and held it up. Immediately, WhizBang sat down. Hershey moved toward Jim, but Matt had him by the leash and yanked him back. Lilli, who never turned down food, lunged forward, but I had her firmly.

"Turn the dogs so they are facing away," Jim said, giving Whiz' leash to Matt. We could hear the buckets being moved.

"You can turn them around," Jim said. "OK, who is first?"

WhizBang could hardly contain himself. He was moving around, trying to keep his butt on the ground but obviously failing.

"OK, Whiz," Jim said, and to Matt. "You can release him."

The dog bolted forward, moved down the line of buckets at lightning speed and knocked over the bucket on the end, gobbling down the treat.

"This is way too easy for him," Jim said. "Turn the dogs around."

The next dog to go was Hershey, who walked quietly past the buckets and without even hesitating, chose the middle one, knocked it over and got the treat.

"Now that you know how the game is played, think you can do this, Lilli?"

He set up the buckets and Lilli headed out. She spent a little more time at each bucket than the other dogs had done, sniffing each one carefully and then chose the one at the end of the line, knocking it over to get the treat."

"Good girl," Jim said.

That was the beginning of our day. After we'd all had a break, Jim handed out hard hats. I learned that my job was to be the victim, which meant that I would have to hide in a tight, hot, spider-infested space in the building while first WhizBang and then Hershey tried to find me. After doing this twice, I was covered with dirt and cobwebs and soaked with sweat.

Jim took a turn, hiding in an upper-story room, and I was astonished at the speed and confidence with which Hershey climbed the ladder to find him. Matt took his turn in a stinky outhouse, and Lilli, with more hesitation and retracing of her steps, finally found him. When we'd done this for a while, all the dogs were rewarded with water and treats and the three of us, sat companionably on the back of the SUV, drinking our own water and watching them play.

"Lilli seems to enjoy this, and I think she's got a nose that can be developed," Matt said looking at me.

I nodded. "She could use this," I said. "Other than our walks at night, she spends most of her time on the couch waiting for me to come home."

Jim turned to me. "I guess Matt told you my story. Border collies are working dogs. Whiz is a different dog when he's doing S & R. There aren't any sheep for him to herd, but he can still find people."

It was now almost noon. We'd been at this for hours and I was getting hungry.

Matt must have had the same idea because he said, "Want to go downtown for lunch? I am starved."

"I'll treat," I said.

"Nope," Matt said. "It's Dutch or nothing."

We found outside tables at Billy's Deli, facing the lake, the dogs, with their water bowls nearby, lying at our feet. It was a beautiful summer day. There were boats on the lake and a nice breeze cooling us. I had changed from my grungy jeans and shirt to a T-shirt and shorts. I couldn't do much about my smell, but at least my clothes were cleaner. I don't think the guys minded; they were as grimy and sweaty as I was.

"We're going to do this again next week," Jim said. "You don't want the dogs to forget what they've learned when a real emergency rolls around."

"How many of you are there in the canine unit?" I asked.

"Just three, but we have lots of volunteers in the community."

"I'm not actually with the canine unit," Jim said. "I'm a detective with the local police. I just do this for a hobby."

I drew a deep breath and looked at the two men. "Thank you for coming to my rescue in the woods," I said. "You saved my life."

Both men nodded.

"Can I ask a question?"

"Sure," Matt said.

"Are you certain you found everyone who was in the woods when the microburst hit?"

Matt sighed and took a sip of coffee. "We do the best we can. We go through the trail registers, check the cars in the parking lots, ask people coming out of the woods if they've seen someone in trouble. We do everything we can to find people."

"I know you do," I said, sensing some irritation in his voice. "And I am very grateful. But what if someone walks into the woods without signing the register? What if someone didn't tell anyone they were going for a walk, so no one called to say they hadn't come home? Maybe that person was someone from out of town, someone who didn't want anyone to know where they were, or someone who wanted to commit suicide in the woods?"

"Suicide by microburst?" Jim said. "Hardly likely. If you were going into the woods to commit suicide, the better time of year would be winter."

"Is this about the ghost?" Matt asked.

I nodded. "She keeps coming back to me. Last week I went to see a medium who told me that I had to find the girl in the woods."

"A medium? Not Madam Celestina. We've had a bunch of complaints about her. I wouldn't believe a word she says," Jim said.

"She seemed convincing," I said lamely.

Jim was shaking his head. "Believe me," he said. "If someone else were still out there, we've had heard about it. Most people don't go into the woods alone without telling someone."

"I told my landlady."

"Well, you were lucky. Very, very lucky. Don't do that again."

"Aye, aye Captain."

Our food had arrived and we ate in silence for a minute. Matt seemed deep in thought, and once he leaned down and patted Hershey's head. Finally he said, "We could just take a walk into the woods, Jim. It would be good practice for the dogs."

"I'm not sure WhizBang could do it," Jim said.

"But he would love it," Matt said.

The two men looked at each other, and at the dogs sprawled at our feet.

"Let me get something," Matt said, standing. Hershey lifted his head and began to get to his feet, but Matt touched his head. "Be right back."

In a few minutes he'd returned with a plastic map, which he spread out on an unused corner of the table. Then he took out a highlighter, and while we continued to eat, he put a large pink circle on the map.

"This is the area of the microburst," he said. "There are lots of unmarked wilderness trails here. Even if you hadn't had the storm, and had gone off the marked trails even once, you could still have gotten lost." He took his marker and made a pink dot. "This is the parking lot for Beaver Lake, where you started into the woods." He made another mark. "And this is where Helmut Aronson died in his tent, right at the edge of the blowdown. Between the parking lot and Helmut's tent, you were following a trail, but beyond that, I'm not sure where you walked."

"I hiked up a small mountain with a steep cliff on one side," I said.

"Possibly Little Cougar. It's more a hill than a mountain, but it has a steep face with lots of thick bushes." He looked at me. "You went down the face of Little Cougar?"

"I did. I thought I saw water below me and a road. My goal was to get to that, but when I got to the base of the hill, the road and water had disappeared."

"The water you were seeing was most likely Juniper Pond." He pointed to the map. "Beaver Lake is in this direction, and has a large tributary flowing into it."

I looked at the space between where I'd entered the woods and Little Cougar. It was such a small space on the map, but in real life it had been an endless area of dense woods.

"Where did you find me?" I asked.

Matt pointed again. "Somewhere around here," he said.

I studied the map. "But there's a road there." I pointed. "How far away is it?"

"About half a mile away."

"I could have died half a mile from a road?"

"We've found people who have died an eighth of a mile from a highway. I don't know how it happens, but it does." He turned back to the map. "The road isn't currently paved because there's only one house on the private land around the pond. The road circles past the pond and then goes up behind a hill. Kids used to go there to smoke dope and make out. I have no idea how far it goes now. Is this the area where you saw the ghost?"

I nodded, looking again at the map. The space between the place where I'd entered the trail and where I'd been found seemed only inches apart. "How could I have gotten so lost?" I said.

"Don't knock yourself up about this, Drew," Jim said. "Some of these areas have spruce as thick as a brick wall." He pointed to the map. "This area between you and the road has a lot of thick woods."

Jim and Matt looked at each other and some secret signal went between them.

"Next weekend then?" Jim asked, looking at me. "Wear what you wore today, but with hiking boots, long pants, a long sleeved shirt and sun hat. And bring lots of water. Keep in mind that the dogs are following a scent so there will be mud, rocks, tree roots, high grass, brambles and bushes, just to name a few things we need to get through."

"Don't forget spiders and dead animals, too," Matt said.

"Sounds lovely," I said. I was no longer working at Adirondack Made and I didn't have to be at the motel until Sunday. I could do Saturday.

"Changing your mind? Remember, this was your idea."

"Absolutely not. When do you want to leave?"

"How about seven, before it gets too hot."

"Can I bring Lilli?"

"Afraid not," Matt said. "Hershey's going to be working and Lilli could be a distraction."

I hoped I wasn't going to be a distraction, or a hindrance. Now that we'd actually agreed to go into the woods again, I was filled with exhilaration, combined with terror. I couldn't wait for Saturday.

Chapter Twelve

On Saturday, I was picked up promptly at seven by Matt. I had gotten up early to give Lilli an extra long walk, but still I felt guilty when I had to close the door on her eager face. Mrs. Steen would come up at one and take her out, but I knew I was depriving my dog of a great walk in the woods.

We drove away from town, a different route this time, but one that was taking me in the direction I'd traveled when I'd set out to walk to Beaver Lake. I tried not to let my anxiety ride shotgun. I was going into the woods again with two guys and two dogs, all of whom knew their way around. But as we got out of the car and headed toward the trail, I started to tremble.

"Wait," I said.

Matt stopped, and seeing what was happening, came over and put his arm around my shoulder. "Breathe, Drew. It's going to be all right."

I nodded, trying to believe his words, but as soon as we entered the woods, I could feel my flashback starting. The woods were all around me, hedging me in, ready to crush me. I would never get out of here, ever and I was going to wander around and around being lost forever. Breathe, Matt had said, but he and the dogs were almost out of sight now, unaware of my panic. Could I really do this?

I took out the orange plastic whistle and blew. Matt, hearing my whistle, stopped, turned around and came back. "OK," he said. "You are going to walk between us. Jim will go first, you will go second, I will go third. Believe me, you are walking with two men who know what PTSD is like."

"Thanks," I said. Starting from a different point in the woods, we were working our way back toward the place where my trip had ended, hoping to finish beside the stream where I had finally lain down, exhausted. I didn't even remember thinking about death then, only the fact that I had been too tired to go on. We reached the stream, with a muddy bank on either side.

"Does this look like the place?" Jim asked.

"I think so," I said. "I was kind of out of it at the time."

"We will assume that this is close enough," Matt said. He took out the sneaker that I'd found in the woods, and which I'd brought with me, allowed the dogs to have a good sniff, and then released them.

Hershey took off through the woods, not following the stream as I had tried to do, but zigzagging between the trees. WhizBang was right behind, his arthritic legs making him slower but gamely working to keep up.

"Come on," Jim said, and we rushed to keep up with the dogs. If it weren't for Hershey's tail waving like a flag in front of us, he would have been hard to see. But WhizBang's black and white color was more visible. We weren't on a trail, so the going was rough. Once I almost tripped on a rock, and another time I banged my foot hard on a root, but having to concentrate on keeping pace with the dogs left no time to stress about being in the woods.

We stepped over an ancient stone wall that marked the edge of what was once a farm field, and were in a meadow that sloped gently upward, and was edged on two sides by woods. Now we were in deep grass that was sometimes wet underfoot, and sometimes uneven so twice I tripped and landed on my knees, soaking both my feet and my pants. I tried not to think about what else might be underfoot. The sun was hot and the mosquitoes fierce, but Hershey was chugging up the hill, his tail waving, and I couldn't stop to find my bug dope. Every once in a while, the dog would halt, put his nose to the air to catch the scent. Then he would take off again, traveling diagonally up the slope of the hill. WhizBang had slowed and I worried about the elderly dog. Would we have to carry the poor thing out? We had almost reached the top of the hill when Hershey stopped. We were still pretty far behind him, and I couldn't see what detained him, but as we drew closer, I saw what appeared to be an ad-hoc dump site: broken furniture, smashed windows still in their frames, mattresses, clothing, car tires and a child's doll littered the ground. Tucked up beside a three legged chair were the remains of a small dog, who must have been hit by a car and come here to die. As the three of us got closer, I saw that Hershey had disappeared, but we could hear WhizBang barking. We followed the sound of barking past the first dump and over the rise. On the other side, mostly hidden by the crown of the hill was a small woods road, and another well-used dump site. An ancient refrigerator sat beside the road, which was really just two ruts through the woods. Hershey and Whiz were beside it. Hershey was sitting patiently. Whiz was barking.

"What have you got, guys?" Matt asked. Whiz pointed with his head at the refrigerator.

Jim took out a bandana and with it wrapped around the handle, tugged on the door of the refrigerator. The door refused to budge. Jim tugged harder and all of a sudden, the door flew open, and a body flopped out onto the ground.

"Oh Christ," Matt said. The smell was overwhelming and I felt my gorge rise. I tried to push it down.

The body, sprawled awkwardly on the ground was that of a teenage girl, possibly sixteen or seventeen.

"I've got to make the call," Jim said, reaching into his pocket for his phone. When he couldn't find cell coverage, he said. "I've got to go back to the car." Reaching into his pocket, he drew out two pairs of plastic gloves. "If you are going to move her, use these." He looked at the ground around the refrigerator, muddied by the footprints of three humans and two dogs. "We'll probably get nothing from this, but don't touch the refrigerator. There might be prints we can use."

"What about WhizBang?" Matt called as Jim turned and started back down the hillside toward the path.

"Keep him here. I'll be back."

Matt took out some treats and gave one to each of the dogs. "Good boy," he said to each of them. Then he took a ball and threw it for Hershey, Whiz trotted after.

"Let's turn her over," Matt said. I put on the gloves and slowly, carefully we turned the girl over.

"Oh God," I said. The girl's face had turned dark and her eyes had sunken into the puffy flesh of her face. Her hair had started to fall out, and she had huge blisters on her face. She was wearing a T-shirt and shorts, but decomposition was pushing her flesh against her clothing. Had this been what Carley looked like when she was found?

A tidal wave of grief rose up in me, and I began to cry, deep gulping sobs. Matt came over and put his arm around me. We moved away from the girl and sat on the grass.

"It's OK" he said gently. "We all react like this sometimes."

"My sister, Carley was killed when I was seventeen. She was visiting my mother in California and had gone shopping downtown. They found her four weeks later at the edge of town. Someone, a stranger, had raped her and strangled her and thrown her in the dump."

I took a deep breath, trying to get my bearings. Hershey came over and put his head on my knee, trying to comfort me, and I patted his glossy brown head. "The last time I saw her, she was all cleaned up and in her casket." Matt nodded, keeping his arm around my shoulder. He was sweaty, and dirty from the trip up the hill, but I didn't mind the smell.

"Look at that?" he said, pointing at the girl. "Her right foot is missing."

"Really?" I stood up and went closer. I was getting used to her smell, but now that she was out of her box, flies had gathered. "It looks like someone just cut it off. Why would they do a thing like that?"

"They're destroying evidence." He looked at the body again. "This girl may be deteriorated too much for the forensic folks to get much, but we have a pretty smart coroner in this town The shoe you found is in your backpack, right?"

"It is," I said. I pulled it out and we looked at it.

"It looks like a shoe for the right foot," Matt said. "It could be hers."

The dogs were back and had settled down beside us on the ground. Scattered in the woods around us were piles of shingles, cut two-by-fours, stacks of tiles, cans of paint, and other building debris.

"Look at this shit," Matt said. "The builders put this stuff here. It's cheaper than paying a dump fee, but who pays for cleaning it up? The town does. It's a disgrace." He stood up and walked back to the crown of the hill, where I could see an ambulance, and a van hurtling toward us, partly hidden by the scrim of trees. I could hear, rather than see the police as they sped up the roadway and then disappeared onto the rough woods road.

A car pulled up in the woods behind us, and Jim got out, with another man in a suit, whom I assumed was the coroner. They moved to where the girl was spread out on the ground. Soon the place was crawling with police, with men taking pictures and mapping out the site, with men standing in knots talking, and others spreading yellow police tape through the trees. In spite of the yellow tape, this murder scene was out in the open and it would probably be impossible to seal from the public. A couple of EMT's in uniform stood at a distance, waiting to carry the body to the hospital for an autopsy.

"I have to be here for a while," Jim said to Matt. "Would you take Whiz home with you? I'll pick him up later." He looked at me. "You need to come to the station today and be fingerprinted and get prints of your shoes made."

"Sure," I said. We turned and headed down the hill. We could have gone down the woods road which ran beside the hill, but the area closest to the murder site was clogged with vehicles. Retracing our steps back down the hill to the trail and the car seemed the best choice. WhizBang walked beside us but kept looking back as if to say, that we'd left someone important behind.

Halfway down the hill, I could see men trudging up to meet us. One carried a heavy video camera on his shoulder, and the other was a little man sweating heavily. These guys weren't police; they were the press.

"Hurry up," Matt said, moving away from the reporter and photographer.

"Hey," one guy called. "I heard there was a murder victim somewhere near the top of this hill. You know anything about that?"

"How the hell do they get the news this fast?" I asked.

"They monitor the police scanner," Matt said.

"Did you hear what I asked?" the guy called again.

"Don't know a thing about it," Matt answered. "We're only taking the dogs for a walk." We moved on. I looked back to see the two men watching us. The man carrying the heavy camera was red-faced and sweating, and his pants were wet from the knees down as though he'd fallen into a puddle. As I turned to look at him, he pointed the camera at me and snapped a picture. Belatedly covering my face, I hurried after Matt and in a short time we were back in the woods.

As we retraced our steps back to the car, I couldn't get the image of the dead girl out of my mind. She'd once been pretty, but a killer had destroyed whatever bright promise her life had once held. Was this the same girl I'd met as a ghost? I didn't know.

"How far we are from where I was found?" I asked.

Matt looked down over the slope of the hill. "Maybe a quarter of a mile. Why are you asking?"

"I was wondering how far a ghost can travel from the place where they died. Madam Celestina, the medium, said that sometimes, when a person dies they get stuck on earth and don't move on."

"I wouldn't know anything about that. Is this the same medium Jim was talking about?"

"She seemed to know things about me that I hadn't told her, like the fact that I was an artist and that my love li...." I looked at him, suddenly embarrassed. "Well she knew things."

"And you believe you were talking to your sister through her?"

"You don't think I should have believed her?"

"There are all kinds of charlatans in this world. Being in the police business puts you in touch with a cartload of them. If it were me, I would have asked for more proof."

"But didn't my story about the ghost convince you to bring the dogs into the woods?"

"Nope."

"Nope?"

"Hershey needed an excuse to be in the woods. Training at an old paper-making plant is fine, but a lot of the people we look for are out here, in the woods and fields. Sometimes I think even the dogs know the difference between practice and a real search. I thought a change of scene would be fun for them."

"It always sounds creepy to say that a dog has fun finding dead people."

"You have to make it fun for them. Otherwise you could never get the dogs to do it."

We had reached the woods. The dogs, off leash, were dashing into the trees and returning breathlessly a few minutes later, only to return to the chase again. Whatever they were following, a squirrel or small mouse was smarter than they were and for them the chase seemed to be more fun than actually catching anything.

We drove to the police station, where I was fingerprinted and had prints of my boots taken. Then Matt drove me home. As I was getting my pack out of the car, Matt said.

"Would you like to have supper some time? You know, dress up in nice clothes, sit at a table with a white tablecloth and maybe a candle. Have some wine and good conversation."

"I'd love it," I said.

"I'll call you."

Chapter Thirteen

When I got back into the apartment, I was greeted enthusiastically by Lilli until she got a scent of the other dogs, then she turned her back on me and lay down in the corner.

"Lilli," I said. "You're my only girl. Come on, let's go out for a walk." A walk is second only to food in Lilli's world, so we got the leash and headed out. I have a trail that I use that skirts part of the lake front and that is close to the apartment. After the hot, dusty, emotionally draining day, I needed fresh air and movement. If I closed my eyes, the decomposing body of the girl rose up. Now I knew what Matt meant by nightmares.

After the walk, I headed back toward the apartment, but as I approached, I saw an unfamiliar van parked in the driveway with the words *The Mountain Journal* emblazoned on the side.

Damn. It was the press. Was it too late to get a room in a motel? Could I camp in the woods for a while? Lilli was tired and began pulling me toward the apartment, when a man opened the door of the van and stepped out. He had a mound of a belly that strained the buttons of his shirt, round glasses and a wattle of flesh under his chin that wobbled when he moved his head. More like a Garden Gnome than a serious journalist. As he approached, he whipped out a pad and pen from his pocket.

"Miss Morgan, Jud Weinstein. Can we talk?"

"I'm busy," I said. "I'm taking my dog in to feed her."

"Just for a minute?"

"NO."

He gave a signal and before I could move another man with a camera was standing in front of me. I turned my head just as he snapped the picture.

"How did you find me?" I asked.

"We saw you coming down the hill and I recognized you as the girl who was lost in the woods. Your address is on file at the newspaper."

Jud took out his wallet, pulled out two twenties and a ten, and holding them toward me asked. "What's your connection to the dead girl?"

Ignoring the money, I said, "There is none. We were just out for a walk and the dogs found her body."

The photographer was trying to snap my picture, but I turned away again. At that moment, Mrs. Steen came out of the apartment house and said, "Madam Celestina told Drew she should find the girl in the woods."

"Sounds interesting," Jud said turning toward Mrs. Steen. "Who's Madam Celestina?"

"A medium. But don't go to her. She's a cheat."

"So you went looking for a dead girl because of a medium?" Jud asked. He was scribbling furiously while the other man snapped pictures of Mrs. Steen.

Jud was holding out the money to Mrs. Steen, who unlike me, didn't refuse. "Tell us about Madam Celestina?"

Mrs. Steen started in. I'm not sure how much she remembered about our visit, so the reporter might not get his money's worth, but I was not going to participate. Instead I went up the stairs to my apartment, poured myself a glass of wine, filled Lilli's food dish and topped off her water, then sat on the couch. Getting Matt and Jim to look for the girl had been the right thing to do, but now it subjected me to something I hated. When I'd come out of the woods, I'd been successful in avoiding the press because I'd been in the hospital, but now that I was well, I had nowhere to hide. I flipped the TV to the local news, where a newscaster was standing in front of the dump, near where we'd found the girl.

"The body of a teenager, approximately sixteen or seventeen was found in a makeshift dump near Juniper Pond, here in the Adirondacks. A preliminary investigation has determined that the teen was strangled. No identification was found on the body, so police are beginning a search for any missing local girl. Anyone having information should contact the following number." A number flashed on the screen. There was a long shot of the hill, and a close up of the junk pile but not the refrigerator. The police chief came on, repeating the number, and asking the public to relay any information they might have about a missing person.

I flicked off the news. It was just a matter of time before Mrs. Steen's story would hit the newspapers and more reporters would be knocking at my door. I had been lucky so far, but what I hadn't realized was that once you've been in the newspapers, you're easy game for anyone.

As I sat on the sofa, Lilli tucked in beside me, I realized that there was probably nowhere in this town I could hide from reporters. I worked in an old motel, and even though there were rooms going empty, my boss would never let me stay there for free. I could fly to California and stay with my mother, but I couldn't do that forever. I had to tough it out. I hoped I had enough fortitude to continue saying no.

My phone rang. It was Matt.

"Have they been to your place yet?"

"I took Lilli for a walk and they were here when I got home. Unfortunately, my landlady is all too willing to spill what she knows to everyone."

"I'm sorry," he said.

"Do you have any suggestions about avoiding the press?"

"I wish I did. They know I'm a forest ranger, but you're the one who's more famous."

"I wish I weren't." I got up and looked out the window to the parking lot below. "I think they've gone, and tomorrow is Sunday, so maybe I can just go someplace where no one knows me."

"Good luck with that. If you need a place to hang out, call me."

"I'll be OK, Matt. But thanks for the offer."

I nuked some supper and sat at a small table away from the window to eat. It was quiet outside, and I didn't want to look out and see that the news van had returned. An hour later, they still weren't back. Maybe I was getting a reprieve.

Chapter Fourteen

The next day was Sunday, a day when I could usually loaf around in my pajamas, make pancakes or scrambled eggs, or better yet, eat a whole pint of Cherry Garcia ice cream and watch sappy movies. After noon I would find a place where Lilli and I could walk, or better yet, walk and take my paints. This morning was different. I kept looking out the window at the parking lot, expecting to see a van sitting there with *The Mountain Journal* printed on the side.

"Come on, Lil, let's go out for breakfast," I said to my dog. She was game for anything, especially if the anything involved getting out of the apartment. My apartment is small: a bedroom, bathroom, and combined kitchen/living room. When I first got here five months ago, I spent a week looking around. I had a little money that I'd saved from my previous job, but even though rents here were much lower than they'd been in New York City, I knew I had to find something cheap. This was cheap. And clean. And quiet, and even though it wasn't spacious, it suited my needs. A month after I got here I got Lilli, or more accurately Lilli got me, having followed me home from a walk through town. She was starved, flea-infested, and had an infected ear where she'd been bitten. It took money that I couldn't afford to bring her back to health, but I never regretted my decision to adopt her. But the consequence of having a dog who spends most of her life in the apartment, was that the place smelled like dog.

I put on a T-shirt, jeans, sneakers and grabbed a sweater. Summer in the Adirondacks is short, and now in mid-August there were already signs that fall was coming. In another month the geese would be starting their flyovers, the boats would disappear from the lake, summer businesses would close or reduce their hours, and the cars that crowded the parking lots of local restaurants would disappear. Usually this happened around Labor Day, so everyone whose livelihood depended on tourists, made the most of these waning economic opportunities.

As I was walking downtown, I thought about what had brought me to Saranac Lake. My father is a painter, and for most of my life, I wanted to paint. I was never as good as he is, even now in his seventies, he can draw a crowd to a gallery just with his name. But he encouraged me to experiment and to be creative.

But after my sister's death, I lost the will to paint. She and I had held onto each other in the days when my parents were screaming at each other, and though my parents had divorced by the time she died, I still considered her my touchstone. Without her I became rootless.

The rootlessness became rebellion. I did drugs, I shoplifted. I acquired a car and drove too fast. I hung around with kids who did all those things, hoping that I could be distracted from the sadness that seemed to have no bottom. Eventually I was arrested when I helped a friend break into a house. The owners were away in Florida and we thought we'd just see what the place looked like. We got stoned, drank their liquor, wrote on their mirrors with lipstick, filled their bathtub with water and bubble bath, and, howled as the water overflowed the tub and pooled on the floor and out into the hallway. When the owners arrived home unexpectedly that evening, my boyfriend and I were having sex in their bed.

We got the charges reduced mainly because we were good kids with no priors, my father was well known, and my boyfriend's dad was a judge. We got community service for six months, and even when we skipped serving meals at the half-way house, or cleaning up trash in the park, nothing really happened.

What changed me? It wasn't the stern lecture from my father whom I neither respected nor liked. I saw my dad as the cause of it all. If he hadn't cheated on my mother, my parents would never have divorced. If my parents hadn't divorced, my mother would never have moved to California and my little sister would not have gone out there to visit, and been killed. He could lecture me until he blew out an artery, but his words made no difference.

What made a difference was a street artist, Jerimiah Callahan, an African- American man in his sixties, who'd been homeless for much of his life, but had, when I met him, been discovered by an avant-garde gallery and was, for the first time, earning a real living.

Jerry loved art and Jerry loved being alive. In spite of a mother who was a crack addict, a father in jail, a wife also in jail and kids in various foster homes, himself the victim of numerous crimes when he was homeless, his art was bright and joyous and decorating every available public space. Jerry made me see that I could use art to speak my anger and pain, and through art, I could move through those things to normalcy.

Lilli and I had reached Billy's Deli, which this morning had a few folks enjoying breakfast. I took a table outside, ordered coffee and an omelet. The waitress brought a bowl of water for Lilli, patted her on the head and pulled a treat from her apron pocket. She set the coffee in front of me.

"Thanks," I said.

My phone rang. I looked at the number. If I don't recognize the number, I don't pick up, but this number had a local area code.

"Lo?"

"Drew," the voice was breathless, as if the person had been running. "I've been trying to reach you. It is very important that we meet."

"Who is this?"

"Celestina. Didn't I say? Drew, something has been happening. Do you remember Molly, the girl we contacted the last time I saw you. She says that she has to talk to you again."

"A ghost is trying to talk with me?"

"A spirit, honey. She is very insistent that I contact you. When can you come to my house?"

"I don't know." It was Sunday, the one day of the week that was my own. I hadn't painted in weeks, and since it was a beautiful summer day, there would be places where I could do a little *plein air*.

"Please," Celestina said. "I'll give you the address."

I rummaged in my purse and found a receipt for groceries and a pen. On the back I wrote her address.

"Come as soon as you can," she said.

"Should I call ahead of time?"

"Yes. Sometimes I'm out doing a reading, but I can postpone those if I know you are coming."

"OK," I said.

As soon as I hung up the waitress appeared with my food, but instead of moving away the woman wanted to talk.

"You're the one who was lost in the woods, ain't you?"

Oh dear, oh dear. I nodded. I wanted to eat my breakfast in peace.

"I saw your pitcher in the paper. Did you see wolves in the woods? People says there ain't wolves up here, but I know they are."

"I didn't see wolves. Lots of blowdown, though. It was hard to move around."

I could see a woman who looked like a supervisor standing near the door watching us. "Lonnie," the woman said.

"What do you think about that girl they found dead? It was a meth overdose, I'll bet. There's lots of that here."

"Lonnie," the supervisor said again.

Lonnie looked up. "Gotta go," she said. "If you go into the woods again, buy a compass."

I already had six compasses in a drawer at home. Maybe I should start wearing them around my neck so people wouldn't push them on me.

I tucked into my egg, sneaking bits to Lilli under the table. The day stretched out ahead of me, a thing I could spend in any way I chose. Lilli and I could take a walk and I could paint some of the old houses in town, or the view across the lake. Then I remembered Celestina's phone call. The last thing I was going to do today was drive over to her house and spend my free afternoon listening to her tale. I had just finished my meal, when I saw someone walking toward me. Damn. Not him again. I yanked Lilli to her feet, grabbed my purse and was headed toward the cashier when he planted himself in front of me, blocking my way.

"Get out of my way, Jud."

"No deal. You're going to talk to me."

I tried to move around him, but he was wider than he was tall and surprisingly agile for one so heavy. Lilli was not one to contest the space and simply sat. A couple of diners, finished with their meals, tried to get past us, and when Jud moved I scooted through the space.

"I'd like to make you a deal," Jud said, catching up with me at the cashier's counter.

"There's nothing I want to say."

"And you don't want to hear about the girl?"

"What do you mean?"

"I have information I'm willing to share. But you need to share with me."

"Why are you doing this?"

Jud was leaning against a support that formed part of the counter. He was red-faced from the heat, and his eyes behind the glasses had a gleam of malice.

"Let me say I think there is a big story here. First, we don't get many murders here in the Adirondacks. Deaths, sure. People get lost and freeze to death in the winter, they drown in the summer, overdose on drugs or hit a deer at night, run off the road and die. These things don't happen often, but they happen. But murder. Murder gets people's attention. I might get a book out of this."

"I don't know anything."

"You are part of this story, Drew. You go to a woman on July twenty-ninth who puts you in touch with your dead sister and a girl named Molly who tells you to find a girl in the woods. Two weeks later they find the girl. You can't tell me there is no connection."

A couple was now standing behind us, waiting to pay. I moved aside to let them get to the cashier.

"Come on Drew," Jud said. "Give me something."

"I don't know anything."

He moved closer and a tidal wave of acrid smell rolled over me.

"You know something, Drew. I know you do. I understand that you don't want your name in the paper, and I promise you will be an anonymous source." People were congregating around us and Jud pulled me toward a table where we sat. He signaled to the waitress for coffee.

"I'll tell you what I know. The police are searching through NamUS the national data base of missing persons and putting the dead girl's DNA into the CODIS system. These things take time, and they have a small department here, but they will find out who she was. The victim was strangled, and as you know, her right foot removed, most likely post-mortem. She's been dead for probably five weeks, so she was likely dead before you went into the woods."

"How do you know these things?"

"I have resources."

"I saw her ghost."

"What?"

"When I was in the woods. I didn't think it was real. I don't even believe in ghosts, and my brain wasn't really working right, but I saw her ghost."

"Wow." He had taken out his notebook and was scribbling in it. "Did she tell you anything about herself, where she came from, what she was doing up here, who killed her?"

I shook my head. "She didn't say anything. Just floated around me."

"I tried to call Celestina, but I had no luck. By the way Celestina is really Agnes Cappelli from Boise, Idaho who was once arrested for running an illegal casino in her house and charging customers to play."

"So you don't think Celestina is legitimate?"

He shrugged. "She's doing this to make money, Drew. She's taking advantage of people who are grieving the loss of a loved one. When you saw her, did she convince you that it was really your sister you were talking to?"

"You sound like a friend of mine. But why would Celestina tell me to 'find the girl,' if she knew nothing about the murder?"

"Good question."

"She called me today. Asked me to come over right away."

"She won't answer my calls. Are you going to see her?"

"I don't want to. To tell you the truth, I would like to have a day when I can paint and not think about death."

He nodded. "I want to go with you when you see her."

"I don't think she'll talk to you, Jud."

"Leave that to me. I can be very persistent, and I think this is a great story."

Chapter Fifteen

The next day was Monday, a work day. I had told Jud that I would call when I decided to visit Celestina, but today would not be that day. My day was going to be long and busy, even though by now the season for tourists in the Adirondacks was winding down. I had just sat down to enjoy my ten minute break when my phone rang. It was Jud.

"You at work?"

"Yup, and you've just interrupted the teeny, tiny break that I'm allowed before I have to return to toilets and unmade beds."

"I'm at Celestina's house but there is no one here. I tried calling her at least five times, but no one answers."

"I thought we were going to go together, Jud. How did you know she would talk to you?"

"I didn't know, but she's part of the story so I just came over. I peeked in the windows," he said. "Tried the doors in case something was open. There is no one here."

"For this you are interrupting my break?"

"Her car is still here in the driveway, Drew. She lives out in the country and there is no way she would go for a walk. There are no sidewalks, not even a trail nearby. She seems to have disappeared."

"I can't help you, Jud. I know nothing about the woman."

"Did you see my article in yesterday's paper?"

"Nope."

"Pick up a copy. I think I did a pretty good job with the story. When the book is finished it might even be Pulitzer material."

"Good-bye Jud."

I walked into the office where they sometimes gave out free copies of the local paper and there in large type was the headline "Local Medium Connected to Girl's Death" over a publicity shot of Celestina. I didn't want to be anywhere near this thing, and was happy I'd not been caught by the photographer. I glanced over the article which seemed to have been mostly provided by Mrs. Steen. Maybe Jud would do a series of articles, though I had no idea where he'd get the material. I wondered if Celestina had seen the paper and to save herself embarrassment, had found a way to disappear, maybe calling a friend to take her away. So far, no one had reported her missing, so I had to believe that being away was not unusual for her.

My phone rang. I could see the boss, Arlette Patchett watching me from the office. There were strict rules here about breaks. I waved at her, stood, dumped my trash in the can and headed toward the next room I was due to clean. My cleaning cart was still in the hallway. I pushed it into the room, shut the door and answered the phone.

"Miss Morgan?"

"Speaking."

"My name is Jennifer Cappelli. My mother is Agnes Cappelli. You would know her as Madam Celestina."

"Yes, I know her," I said warily. "But I haven't seen her for a couple of weeks."

"She called me last week. Said it was important she talk to you. Have you heard from her lately?"

"She phoned me yesterday when I was at lunch. She wanted me to come over as soon as I could to talk to her."

"So you haven't seen her since?"

"Nope."

"I hate to bother you, but I'm worried. Every Monday I take my Mom out to lunch and then Bingo. We never miss a date, but this morning when I went to her house, she wasn't there, and her car was still in the driveway. My mother never goes anywhere, except to give a reading. She has arthritis, so she doesn't go for walks, and she has very few friends. In fact, I have called every one of her friends and each person says they haven't seen her. You and I are only talking now because she called me about you."

"Have you called the police?"

"Not yet. A person has to be missing for twenty-four hours before they will start looking. I wish she would tell me if she is just going to take off like that."

"I'm sorry," I said. "I wish I could help."

I heard movement outside the room and then a knock. It might be one of the other maids wanting to borrow something from the cart, or it might be the boss checking up on me.

"Sorry," I said. "I've got to go."

I didn't hear from Jennifer for the rest of the week and there was nothing in the paper about the missing woman so I assumed that Celestina had been found.

On Saturday afternoon, I was looking through the dresses in my closet, trying to find something to wear on my dinner date with Matt. I wanted it to be flirty, but sending the message that we were just getting to know each other. Lilli knew that something was up, and she wasn't going, so she assumed her space on the couch and eyed me accusingly.

A knock on the door. It was Matt, wearing a light grey jacket with a red tie and pressed jeans. Jeans probably meant that we weren't going to somewhere really fancy, or they meant that this was a man who wore jeans everywhere. But he looked so nice, and smelled so nice I was willing to cut him some slack.

"Ready?"

I nodded. He walked me around to the passenger side of the car, held open the door and I got in. "Where are we going?"

"There is a new French restaurant near Lake Placid. I thought we could try it."

We headed out. The sun was just setting on the lake, splashing pinks and reds across the sky and the darkening water. The trees were now in silhouette, and the distant mountains were fading into darkness.

"Celestina's daughter called me last week. She said her mother has gone missing." I looked over at Matt. "Did Jim Weims say anything to you about that?"

He shook his head.

"If the police are looking for a missing person, don't they publicize it in the paper?"

He shrugged again. "To tell you the truth, kids and old people get the most attention. Especially old people with some sort of dementia. Did Celestina's daughter say her mom was forgetful?"

"No. But her car was still in the driveway, and she lives out in the country. Her daughter said it was unlikely that she would walk anywhere."

"I wouldn't worry about it too much. I'm sure she will show up soon. The cops may have gone to the house and determined that nothing was wrong. But why do you care anyway? You two aren't related."

A sliver of anger shot through me. It was true that I did not know the woman, and I had no personal stake in where she'd decided to go, but her words had pushed me to find the girl in the woods. She'd been partly responsible for the discovery of a murder. But, I was on a date with a nice guy, an event that hadn't happened in a long time and I didn't want to spoil it by bringing up a subject that we would argue about. We drove in silence for a while and eventually pulled up in front of a single-story stone building, with fairy lights strung around the door and windows. A sign in the shape of a sheep read 'Chez Mouton.' We went in and were in a large low-ceilinged room. A huge fieldstone fireplace with a fire burning in it filled one side of the room. On each table were lit candles and along the mantelpiece of the fireplace were fairy lights. There were about twelve tables in the place, but only four of them had diners sitting at them. A maitre 'd approached us.

"We have a reservation," Matt said. The man nodded.

"This is beautiful," I said when we were seated. I reached out and touched Matt's hand. "Thank you."

"Well, I thought you deserved something better than slogging through waist-high grass, or hiding in a buggy hole waiting to be sniffed out."

"I should be the one buying you dinner," I said. "I did promise you that."

He nodded. He was looking at the drinks menu. The waiter was standing, waiting.

I looked at the menu. Normally I would have a glass of white wine but this was a special date.

"Sangria," I said.

"Stout," Matt said.

"So, tell me, Miss Morgan. What brought you to the Adirondacks?"

"How do you know I'm not from around here?"

"Because I grew up around here and I know almost everyone in town. I would certainly know if I'd seen you before."

"You know *everyone* in town?"

"Almost everyone. The winter population is very small, and because some of the summer people come every year, I've gotten to know them too. But you haven't answered my question."

"I was a graphic artist for a little company called Alhambra Studios in New York City. We did advertising for the entertainment industry."

"So you've always been an artist?"

"My father is. My mother is a lawyer."

"Wait. Your father is R.S. Morgan? I think I've seen some of his stuff, very modern, with lots of color. I've only seen him in books, not in person."

"That's him. Some of his paintings can cover an entire wall. We had a house in Brooklyn where his studio was on the top floor and sometimes the smell of paint would permeate the whole house. So, how about you? You grew up here?"

"Wanakena. But I love the woods, and I love animals and when I got out of the service, those two seemed like a fit for me. I had to go back to school to work for the DEC, but I've never been sorry I decided to be a ranger."

Our waiter had arrived with the drinks and was standing, waiting for us to order. When we had finished ordering, we continued to talk. I told him about coming up to Saranac Lake to spend August with my grandparents who had a summer camp here.

"So what's a ranger's life like?"

He took a sip of his drink and imperceptibly began the transformation from a guy having a casual dinner with a girl, to woods cop.

"I have two jobs. I protect the environment from the people and I protect people from the environment. For instance, if a bus carrying forty people pulls into the parking lot at the Garden in the High Peaks Wilderness, I know there are going to be people jamming the trails. We do have rules about that, but if no one is there to enforce them, we'll have people backed up on the trails, pushing past each other to get around, and if its muddy, subjecting that ground to erosion. Well, you've heard some of my stories already."

"Did you always love being in the woods?"

"Yup. But it wasn't until I was seventeen and worked for a summer for my father that I realized being indoors wasn't the life for me. I remember sitting at a desk, looking out at the trees and realizing that my real life should be out there."

"What do you do for fun?"

"You mean besides working with Hershey on the weekend? Last summer I got two weeks off and Hershey and I went West in my little camper. I saw Bryce, Arches, Yosemite, Yellowstone. I couldn't do much hiking because dogs aren't allowed on National Park trails, but we had a great time just the same. How about you? What do you do for fun?"

"When I was in the city, I used to like eating out, and going to the movies. There was so much there to do. Since I've been here, all I do is work and spend time with Lilli."

"Why did you leave New York?"

Was it confession time?

"Something made you unhappy with the city," he prompted.

"I had an affair with a married man. One day he was telling me he and his wife weren't sleeping together and it was only a matter of time before we'd be married, and two weeks later, I was watching him and his pregnant wife having coffee together at a local restaurant."

Matt was silent. "My wife and I talked about having kids. At least that was the plan before I went to Iraq, but when I got home, I was still waking at night, trembling and sweaty, and even something as benign as a car backfiring would send me rushing to be inside. I couldn't hold a job, because the smallest thing would push me back into the dust, the heat, the dead bodies of my friends and the constant terror. When we divorced, we realized it was probably a good thing we'd never reproduced."

"Does your wife live around here?" It seemed like a personal question, but I had to know. I wasn't going to fall in love with a married man again.

He shook his head. "She's happy with her new husband in Arizona and I'm happy here." He reached forward and took my hand. "When I saw you in the woods, you were worn out, starving, dirty and battered but pushing yourself to stay alive. Not many people could have done what you did. That was when I realized I wanted to get to know you."

We sat talking and eating for several hours more and at ten, Matt drove me home. I thought about inviting him in for a drink, but my apartment was so small and cluttered that I changed my mind. I got out of the car, and he walked me to the door.

"I'd invite you in, but…" I said.

"It's OK." He moved closer. "I had a nice time, Drew. Call me when you want to treat me to that steak dinner."

"Is that how you see me? A free steak?"

"Who am I to pass up free food?" He reached forward and ran his thumb down the side of my face and then moved in closer and kissed me. Oh God. This was a man I could fall for. We kissed long and passionately. I could smell his aftershave and the manly smell under it. I wondered what he looked like without his clothes. No. No. This was way too new to be thinking that way.

Then he pulled away. Maybe he was also thinking that we needed to give this time. He turned and walked toward the car. "I'll call you," he said.

I waved back, then turned, went in the door and climbed the stairs to my apartment where Lilli was waiting to greet me. I looked around at the single room that is my living/dining room. There were magazines on the chairs, and Lilli's toys scattered around the floor. If I were going to invite a man home, I needed to give this place a good cleaning. Did I want to invite this particular man home? Yes. I decided. I certainly did.

Chapter Sixteen

As I was beginning to learn, Autumn comes early to the Adirondacks. It was still late August, but already the trees were starting to turn and the summer visitors, like the birds, were heading to warmer climates. When I got to work on Tuesday morning, Arlette Patchett the owner/boss called me into her office, a grubby little space which smelled strongly of cigarettes, Arlette's unapologetic habit.

"Drew," she said, motioning me to a chair. "We need to talk."

'I need this job, I need this job,' I said to myself, but I waited.

"You know that things have been slow. They always get slow when we go into winter. I'm afraid I can't afford two girls working here."

"You're going to fire me?"

She sat back in her chair, took a long drag from her cigarette and nodded. I barely heard her next words, something about my hours being cut from five days a week to two, Thursday and Friday.

"I'm sorry," she said. I wasn't sure if she really was.

I moved out into the lobby of the hotel in a daze. No one was around so I got my cart and began pushing it down the corridor. The other maid had her cart parked at right angles to me and, when I tried to pass, she smiled cruelly. She'd been here for at least ten years and was going to keep her job. Ten years working in a motel. I would have gone crazy. But working in a motel was a job, and lots of people in this area were struggling. I knew nothing about the other maid's life, but I'd seen two little boys hanging around her in the afternoons when she was cleaning, so I assumed she was a single mom. I should not be angry that she would still be working, while I wasn't.

After my shift was over, I stopped by Adirondack Made to say hi to Mary Ellen and to learn whether any of my paintings had sold.

"We sold a few of your cards," she said. "But nothing else. Things have been very, very slow. I'm thinking of shutting down a month early. If I'm paying heat and rent and earning nothing I might be better off in Florida."

We were sitting at a table in the back, drinking coffee. Suddenly Mary Ellen got up and went to the counter, returning with a piece of paper. "Last week a man came around with these posters. They are looking for artists to teach in an after-school program at the high school. This might be right up your alley, Drew."

I looked at the poster. They were looking for teachers for three afternoons a week, Monday, Tuesday and Wednesday from three until four-thirty. There was no mention of pay, but at this point I was willing to take anything. The job would start at the beginning of September. It might not be much, but it was something.

"I also saw an ad for a job in the window of Billy's Deli," Mary Ellen said.

"They're hiring this time of year?"

"It's not for the Deli. Billy's sister, Janet is starting a catering business, doing parties for special occasions, and they're looking for waiters and waitresses. It might be something to look into."

I nodded. I would go over to Billy's right now, and then I would go home and call the school and last, my father. I might be able to stay here after all.

Billy took my application and said that Janet would call. This was a new business, so he wasn't sure how many gigs Janet would get, but I had several things going for me. I was clean, un-pierced and seemed to be reasonably mature. "You can't imagine the kids who come in here looking for work," Billy said.

I went home to Lilli, who wanted to walk. On our stroll around town, I called the school and was put in touch with the guidance counselor who said that since they'd cut the art teacher's job, there had been lots of requests for an art program. I was the first one who'd called since they'd put out the posters. Could I e-mail them a resume and contact information? And, if they liked what I sent, could I start on September 5, which was about a week away?

"Sure," I said, feeling better about my prospects.

Last, I called my dad.

"Drew," he said. "It's great to hear from you. Are you still up there in the wilds of Maine?"

"The Adirondacks, Dad. Yup, I'm still in New York State but about three hundred miles from you."

"I couldn't figure out why you left a good job here in New York to go all the way up there."

"It's quieter, and cheaper than living in the city."

"What are you doing for work?"

"Selling my stuff in a local store and I'm in personal service."

"Personal service. What the hell is that?"

"Working in a motel."

"Waiting tables? Making beds?"

"Things get slow here when winter comes. I lost my job selling art, so yeah, I'm making beds for a living. But I might be teaching art to high school kids."

"Great. Sounds like the perfect entry-level job for an artist. You don't want to come back to the city?"

"That was what I wanted to talk to you about. I'm thinking of coming back. Could I stay with you while I find a job?"

There was a long pause. This didn't sound good. Finally he said "I'll have to run this by Tina."

I didn't ask who Tina was, no doubt one of a long line of young women whom my father slept with and then discarded like Kleenex. If he needed to check in with Tina about whether I could move back home, she might be more permanent than most of his women.

"I won't be any trouble, Dad. Give me a broom closet or the couch in the TV room. I'll be out as soon as I can afford a place of my own."

"Let me get back to you on this."

Shit. It didn't look good. We said good-bye and I hung up. I looked down at Lilli who had found something fascinating at the base of a tree. If I did move back to the city, what would I do with a dog I loved? I would not give her up to the shelter, and lots of landlords didn't like dogs. Shit, again.

The other option, probably my last, would be to open up my own small advertising agency, but that might take capital I didn't have, and I might be dealing with a seasonal clientele. That, at least, might let me stay here. I turned toward home. Geese flew overhead, and a car went by, with someone inside honking and waving at me. I didn't recognize the occupant, but lots of people had gotten to know me through Adirondack Made, even saying hello in the grocery store. It wasn't like the five years I'd been in New York City where even the neighbors in my apartment complex scarcely lifted their heads when our paths crossed. It would be hard to leave here. Why did life have to be so difficult?

Chapter Seventeen

When I got back to my apartment, I booted up my computer and Googled 'graphic artist,' but most of the jobs were in Watertown or Syracuse, not the Adirondacks. I would be in a city again, barely able to afford my rent and dealing with noise, and potential violence. I would not have a landlady who could sometimes take care of my dog and I would not be able to see the lakes, rivers and mountains that I'd grown to love. If I were going to be in Syracuse or Watertown , I might as well go back to New York City.

I turned off the computer, and rummaging around in my art stuff, found a notebook where I began jotting down ideas for an art class. These kids were teens, so the lessons had to be fun, but challenging. I would have to buy supplies. Would the school pay for them? How many weeks would the class run? Were kids going to be required to sign up for the whole series, or would I have fifteen kids the first week and five on week two? All of these were questions I needed to ask. But first I needed to get the job.

I took out my sketch pad and drew Lilli sleeping on the floor. She rolled over on her back, her eyes closed, her paws bent at the ankles. Her *Naked Maja* pose. Maybe I could use her as a model. None of the parents would then complain about my using nudes with school kids, and I'd have no tittering from the boys or girls. When I'd been in art classes, we'd spent a lot of time talking about color theory, and line and shadow. We studied the great masters: Picasso, Van Gogh, Modigliani, but I didn't think kids today cared about those artists. If I were lucky, I might get young people with some real talent, kids whom I could inspire, and who might like me as a teacher. Last, I wrote up a resume, printed it off and e-mailed it to the address given me by the guidance counselor.

I took out my watercolor paper and did a few small sketches of the winter woods. Snow on a tree with a bright cardinal as a decoration, Christmas balls on a bed of firs with a chickadee, the stuff that people in this area wanted. I did a couple of sketches from photographs I'd taken of bright fall trees against a blue sky. I could develop these into paintings and cards, and offer them for sale at the "Shop Local" event near Christmas. That event, with snow sculpture, snowmobile races, wood chopping competitions and fireworks, always attracted a lot of people and gave local businesses one last infusion of cash to get them through the winter.

When I looked at the clock it was close to ten-thirty. I might take some time in the next few days to see what was available in Lake Placid. In addition to bigger hotels in the area, there was the Whiteface Mountain Ski Center which might need extra winter help. Finally, most of the problems that seemed so intractable earlier in the day, now seemed manageable. I changed into my pajamas, climbed into bed and in a short time I was asleep.

I dreamed I was walking through the woods on a beautiful fall day, enjoying the air on my face, the smell of the trees around me, the bird call. I could hear someone behind me, coming up fast. I turned to look, but instead of passing me the man stopped. Suddenly he was pushing me against a tree, his hands around my neck, choking me. I was fighting him but he was stronger than I was. I tried to breathe. I was losing air, losing ground, losing my life.

I woke in a sweat with Lilli tucked up against me, snoring. Climbing carefully out of bed, I went to the kitchen to make coffee. It was four-thirty, much too early to take Lilli out and with lots of time stretching out before me until I needed to be at work. Through the back garden I could see lights winking at the base of the cedar trees, probably car headlights on an adjacent street. I thought about the dream. Most of my dreams take the form of being lost somewhere, but this was more violent. Maybe it was just the worry of losing one job and trying to find another. Thinking about my anxiety, reminded me that I needed to go and see Celestina. I had her daughter's number and could call to see if she'd returned home, but it was way too early in the morning for phone calls.

At eight o'clock I was in my uniform, ready to head out to work when the phone rang. It was an unfamiliar number but the area code was right so I picked it up.

"Miss Morgan?" The voice was unfamiliar.

"Yes?"

"This is Jay Johnson. I'm the principal of the high school. I understand that you are interested in job teaching art to our kids."

"I am," I said.

"We're impressed with your resume. Can you stop by the high school this afternoon at three so we can meet, and I'll give you the details about the class."

"I got the job?"

"You did. We are really delighted that you can do this. The job will run for ten weeks at the beginning and then we'll see how it goes. We have raised some funds to pay you, and I have to say that there's a great deal of enthusiasm for this. I am looking forward to meeting you."

He had set the appointment up for three, but my motel job didn't end until three-thirty. "Can we meet at four?" I asked.

"Sure. See you then."

My second call came as I was driving to work. It was Billy's sister, Janet who said she wanted to hire me for a party at the end of September. She was already booking parties for December and January. Would I be around then?

September sounded good and though December seemed years away, it was a job.

"Sure," I said.

Chapter Eighteen

It was the last day of August and school wasn't in session yet. But when I got to the school, lots of teachers were in their classrooms, putting up bulletin boards, counting books, writing in their plan books or just sitting at their desks, drinking coffee. When I knocked on Jay Johnson's door, he was on his knees behind his desk, cleaning up some spill on the floor. He rose to greet me, a forty-something man, tall and trim with a receding hairline and horn-rimmed glasses. He was wearing jeans and a sweat shirt, not his usual principal attire and he seemed like the best kind of administrator, kindly, approachable, forgiving. I wondered if I'd ever encountered a potential boss like him.

We spent twenty minutes talking about the class period, three to four-thirty, Monday, Tuesday and Wednesday and the pay, more per hour than I was making in the motel. I signed papers so I could be put on the payroll and then Jay rose.

"Let me show you the room," he said. He led me down the hallway and unlocked a door. He flicked on the lights and I could see that this had once been a room with a lot of resources. "How sad for these kids, that this room isn't used any more," I said.

"It is. Supplies are relatively cheap, but teachers aren't. We have to pay our teachers not just a salary but health insurance and retirement."

I would get only an hourly salary, but it was better to have the job than nothing at all and teaching kids might be more fun than working in a motel.

He was opening cupboards, revealing stacks of drawing and watercolor paper, tubes of acrylic and watercolor paints, mannequins, tubs of clay, brushes, pencils, charcoal, and erasers. A potter's wheel sat against one wall, next to a dozen wooden easels. A cork bulletin board, holding a lone notice about a 2013 art show took up all the space along one wall. I'd had a few art classes, but most of what I'd learned had been from my father. If I'd had a class in a room like this, would I have become a better painter?

"So, you'll start on the 6th?" Jay asked. "I know it doesn't give you much notice, but the kids are so eager for this class."

I nodded. "How long have you been advertising this job?"

"A month. We should have started earlier, but the grant just came through." He reached forward and shook my hand. "I am so glad we have you on board, Miss Morgan."

On the sixth of September, my first teaching day, I got to the classroom early so I could wrestle a soft chair up to the front of the classroom. Putting a blanket on the chair, I got Lilli to climb up into it. Maybe it was too much to ask the kids to draw my dog, but I wanted to see what they could do. I laid out sheets of drawing paper on each desk and put a supply of sharpened, number 4B pencils on the desks along with erasers. As an afterthought, I added some vine charcoal. We'd start the class with a few gesture drawings. Lilli didn't do tricks, but with treats I could get her into different poses. Then I took a deep breath. I've never taught art before and I've had very little contact with teens, but I love being an artist and I hoped that this enthusiasm would, like a bottle on the tide, carry me forward.

At three on the dot they filed in. There were ten of them, most of them sixteen or seventeen, a few as young as thirteen. They looked at me and without a word took their seats. Some of them had drawing pads with them and one boy, a kid with long hair and a stained T-shirt, took out his pencils and immediately started to sketch Lilli.

"I am Miss Morgan," I said, looking at the kids. "But call me Drew. I'm very happy to be here and I think we are going to have a good time making art." I read through the list I'd been given. Everyone was here. It might take me a while to learn names, so I resolved to put name tags on my list of supplies. When we'd finished with the attendance, I pointed to Lilli. "We're going to start with some gesture drawings. I'll put on the timer for three minutes and I want you to draw without looking at your paper. Remember, this is just a warm up, so just give me an outline of the dog without too many details. You should be spending more time looking at the dog than you do looking at your paper. I have extra pencils and erasers here if you need them, or if you want to try these exercises in charcoal, go for it."

"What's your dog's name?" a girl in the back row asked.

"Lilliput," I said. "I call her Lilli. OK, are you ready? Start."

I looked at the kids, who had started to draw. Some of them clearly had done this before. The boy with the long hair who'd started drawing the minute he sat down, already had a good likeness of Lilli.

We did three gesture sessions, three minutes each. I walked around, looking at what the kids were doing. Some of these teens were very good, others seem to be struggling, but no one complained. It was really too bad that the art program had been cut, but then if it were still going, I wouldn't have had a job. After the gesture drawings, I gave Lilli a treat and then got her to lie down again.

"Now's your chance to do a larger drawing," I said. "Take your time. I am not here to grade you, so just do your best."

The room was quiet as the kids worked. I wondered if the other teachers had kids who were so eager to participate. It might be that after six weeks of class, these kids would be sick of me too, but right now, teaching was a joy. I walked around the room, helping a few students work out proportion and shading. I stopped by the kid with the long hair to see what he was doing. His drawing was wonderful. He'd not only gotten the proportions and the shading right, but he'd gotten the expression on Lilli's face."

"You're very good," I said. He looked at me.

"Darryl, isn't it? Darryl Boxer?"

He nodded.

"I mean it," I said, bending down so we were face to face. "You have real talent."

"My dad says I need to learn a trade, like welding or somethin'. But I like doing this."

I took out my cell phone and scrolled through my pictures. Then I put the phone beside him so he could see my father's latest creation, a ten-foot by twenty-foot painting of the ocean, which he called "Rip Tide."

"My father is a professional artist," I said. "This painting, which was purchased by some Chinese millionaire, sold for twenty thousand dollars."

"Jesus," he said.

"Would you be willing to let me take pictures of your work? I'll send it to him. He might give you some leads on art galleries."

"Seriously?"

"Why not. You're good. He might be able to help you."

He nodded and I snapped a photo of his drawing of Lilli.

He flipped a page in his drawing pad. The picture was of Mirror Lake with the mountains behind it. He flipped again. A cat on a sidewalk, its body spread out, a smile on its face. Another picture, this one of a girl and suddenly I realized that I knew who she was, although the last time I'd seen her, she'd been lying dead. It had been two weeks since the body had been found and the police had just released the news that the girl's name was Sara Kyzinski. Sara, not Molly.

"Is she a friend of yours?" I asked.

"Sort of. We weren't dating exactly, just hanging out together."

"She's the girl who was killed, wasn't she?" I asked.

He nodded.

"Was she a student here?"

"Nah. She was from somewhere in Pennsylvania. She worked at a hairdressing place here in Saranac and waited tables in Lake Placid."

"Can I take a picture of your drawing?"

"You ain't gonna show it to no one?"

I shook my head. It was hard to lie to this kid, but I needed to talk to Jud Weinstein, my reporter friend.

We spent the last fifteen minutes making a list of what the kids wanted to study, and then the kids filed out.

"Miss Morgan?" a girl asked. She was standing alone near the door after the others had left.

"Drew," I said.

"Don't pay attention to Darryl. He's just weird."

"Thank you…" I'd forgotten her name.

"Janelle," she said. I needed to spend some time with these kids.

She turned, but before she could leave I caught up with her. "Janelle," I asked. "Have the police been around here asking questions about the girl who was killed. Sara Kyzinski?"

She nodded.

"Did any of you know her?"

"She hung out with Darryl sometimes, but it was like we were---you know---just hicks to her. She thought she was better than us. I didn't like her much myself." Janelle glanced away. "I was sorry she got killed and all, but it wasn't like she was from around here."

When I got home, I called Jud. "Can we go out for a beer?" I asked. "I have something I want to share."

"What have you got?"

"I'll show you when I see you."

We met at a small bar/restaurant where the locals hang out. It wasn't fancy, but it had an upstairs room that was mostly empty because the servers had to hike up a narrow set of stairs to deliver food or drinks.

When we'd got our drinks, I got out my cell and pulled up Darryl 's picture of Sara.

"Darryl Boxer, the boy who drew this picture, said he knew her. She didn't go to school, but instead worked part-time for a local hairdresser and waitressed a bit."

"How long had she been in the area?"

"He didn't say. But this is definitely the girl who was murdered. I saw her body."

He pulled the phone closer and stared at it. "Pretty," he said.

I took my phone back. "So what have you got?"

"Patsy's been fired."

"So?"

"Patsy's my girlfriend. She works, *worked* as a secretary in the police department."

"She was the one feeding you information?"

"Uh huh."

"Before Patsy left did she tell you what the police had found?"

"The girl came from Scranton, Pennsylvania. Jim Weims and another cop went down there last week to talk to the parents."

"Do you have an address for the parents?"

He shook his head. "But there's always the internet," he said.

I could talk to Matt about the case, but he probably wouldn't tell me anything. The other puzzling aspect in all this was that Celestina had said the dead girl was named Molly, but Darryl had called her Sara. Were we talking about a single murdered girl with two names or were we talking about two girls?

"I'd like to talk to Darryl," Jud said. "Do you know where he lives?"

"You can't do that," I said. "I promised him I wouldn't show the picture to anyone. You'll need to find another way around this."

"OK," he said. "Patsy didn't tell anyone in the department that she was sharing her notes with me, or I might find myself out of a job too." He leaned back in his seat, his chubby belly looming out in front of him. "To tell you the truth, I'm sick of this town, sick of these people and definitely sick of winter. Maybe I'll move to Florida and become a car salesman."

"What about 'murder gets people's attention.' What about the Pulitzer? What about the best seller? "

"Screw those."

"You can't just give up," I said, reaching forward and gripping his moist hand. "We need to find out who killed this girl."

"The police can do that," he said. "What do you care? She wasn't a relative or anything."

"No, she wasn't. But she wanted me to find her. We did that, and now I've got to help find her killer."

"So what do you want to do?" he asked. "Drive to Pennsylvania and talk to the parents? If the police learn what we're doing, we could be arrested for interfering with an active investigation."

"If you're going to be an investigative reporter, Jud, you need to take chances, stick your neck out. Nobody wins a Pulitzer sitting at home waiting for information to come waltzing up the driveway."

He took a sip of his coffee, thinking about it. Why had I ever hitched myself to this loser? Finally, he said. "All right. When do you want to leave?"

I thought about my schedule. Starting next week, I would be at the motel Thursday and Friday and at the school Monday, Tuesday and Wednesday. That left Saturday and Sunday free. "How about Saturday? It will take us most of a day to drive down there, and we'll have to get a motel room."

"Two rooms," he said. "And I've seen that old wreck you drive. We'll take my car."

"I want to take my dog," I said. "I can't leave her alone for two days."

"What happened to your dog when you were lost in the woods?"

"That was different. I didn't have a choice and my landlady fed her."

"OK," he said.

"She's a good girl. She won't be any trouble."

The only fly in the ointment turned out to be Matt who called me on Thursday asking if I'd like to go out with Hershey and WhizBang on Saturday. I told him I was driving down to New York City for the weekend to see a girlfriend and I wouldn't be back until late Sunday. Could we postpone this a week? He sounded disappointed, which was nice. I was disappointed too, but my trip to talk to the parents of the murdered girl was more important.

Chapter Nineteen

I had come on this trip armed with snacks and water for myself and Lilli. Before this, I'd never spent more than half an hour with Jud, so being in the close environment of the car gave me a whole new appreciation for his laxness regarding hygiene. Thank goodness it was still warm enough to open the windows. The other issue was Jud's fondness for country and western music: Patsy Cline, Merle Haggard, Johnny Cash, Tammy Wynette, Eddy Arnold and Willy Nelson. He put in a CD and then sang along off key and at top volume. I'm not a music snob, in fact I think my taste is pretty liberal but after an hour of hearing about hosses, pick-ups and lonely widders I was ready for something else.

"Do you have any other CD's?" I asked.

"Yeah sure." He reached across me and began fumbling in the glove box.

"I'll get that," I said, since he had his eyes less on the road than on what he was looking for. I drew out a stack of CD's. Tim McGraw, Kenny Chesney, Blake Shelton, Brad Paisley, Trace Adkins. Oh for some Cher, Adele, Madonna or Beyonce. I fished around but none of those were available.

"Maybe we could take a break from the music," I said, looking out at the scenery. The woods of the Adirondacks had given way to farm fields dotted with cows and the occasional small town. "What do you suppose brought a girl like Molly up to northern New York?"

"Molly? I thought her name was Sara." He looked at me. "What is it?"

"Darryl said her name was Sara. Madam Celestina called her Molly."

"But the girl in the picture *was* the dead girl."

"She was. And the cops talked to the parents in Scranton."

"They did," he said.

"Two forty seven Linden Avenue is the address you found for Ralph and Emily Kyzinski on the internet?"

"It was the only address under that name." Jud said.

We had to be on the right track. Both of us were putting out a considerable outlay of time and money to follow up on something that might or might not be real. Jud was silent for a while. Maybe he was thinking the same thing. Were we making a terrible mistake?

Lilli began to move restlessly and then growl softly. "There's a rest area in two miles," I said. "My dog and I both need a pee. Pull off there."

"Can you do some of the driving?"

"Sure," I said. "Just let me get some coffee, and I'll take over."

We reached Pennsylvania in late afternoon, having stopped twice at rest areas to load up on coffee and empty the accumulation in our systems.

The house owned by Ralph and Emily Kyzinski sat on a quiet dead end that might have had new housing in the old days, but was now inhabited by downtrodden wrecks interspersed by empty buildings with long grass hiding the walkway, peeling paint, sagging roofs and the general look of neglect.

Number 247, our goal, seemed to be inhabited if a rusty Ford pickup parked in the driveway could be believed. There was no answer when I knocked. I knocked again.

"Yeah?" The door was yanked open by a balding man in his fifties, who was dressed in a dirty sleeveless undershirt and stained khakis. You could light his breath with a match.

"Mr. Kyzinski, I'm Drew Morgan and this is my colleague Jud Weinstein."

"You cops?"

I shook my head. "Could we talk to you and your wife for a minute?"

"I already talked to the cops. You sure you ain't more cops?"

"We aren't police," Jud said.

"OK, then," Kyzinski said, moving from the doorway and leading us into the hallway. On one side was a stairway to the upstairs and on the other was a doorway to the living room. A TV was blaring and on the coffee table was a half-filled bottle of scotch and a glass. Along one wall was a floor-to-ceiling stack of cardboard boxes. On a table sat a computer with the e-Bay logo on the screen. The whole house smelled of alcohol and decay.

"I work as a cleaner midnight to seven," Ralph said. "I was just going to bed."

"Is your wife available to talk with us, Mr. Kyzinski?" I asked.

"We're divorced," he said. "She's in Oregon. I ain't seen her for more than five years." He settled onto a sofa and waved us toward two straight chairs. "You want to talk about Sara? The cops from New York was already here. I already took time off from my job to go see the body and make the arrangements. You ain't asking me to go up there again, are ya?"

"I'm so sorry for your loss."

"Yeah," he said.

"Can you tell us a little bit about your daughter?"

"How come you're here asking all these questions? When she went missing, I called the police, and they come out here, but nothing ever happened. I think they dropped the ball. And now that she's dead, I got cops up the wazoo. First the local police, then the New York police and now you guys."

It was time to come clean. "I'm not police," Jud said. "I am a reporter for a newspaper in Saranac Lake, the place where your daughter died. I would like to write a story about your daughter. Sara was, I am sure, the bright light of your life, someone who had her whole future ahead of her. No one as beautiful as she was should have died like that. When I've written my book about this case, everyone will know what a remarkable young woman she was."

I thought he was laying it on a little thick, but Ralph didn't flinch. He got up from the couch and brought over a framed picture. The girl in the photo, Sara, had wide blue eyes, a straight nose, soft lips and long, straight, blonde hair. The perfect teenager.

"She coulda' been a model," Ralph said. "And I guess she wanted that. But I didn't have no money to pay for a trip to New

York City which was where she wanted to go." He lapsed into silence.

"How long has Sara been gone?"

He sighed and ran his hand through his thinning hair. "She left here on June 9th, but I thought she'd gone to stay overnight with a friend."

"She did that often?"

"Often enough. Two days later I called the friend's Mom who tells me Sara was never there. I got a little panicked and talked to the police. So then they starts to look for her."

"How long did they look for her?"

"A couple weeks, a month mebbe. They thought she mighta met someone on the internet, but Sara didn't keep nothin' on her computer. She sent all her messages through SharpChat on her phone."

"Snapchat. The messages are erased almost as soon as they are sent. Did they ever find her phone?"

"Nope."

"I am sorry," I said.

Jud was looking at the pile of boxes in the corner of the room. "What's all this?" he asked.

"Sara's stuff. I'm selling it. You heard of 'Molly Bee'? That was her. She started out when she was three, coached by her mother, and by the time she was in sixth grade she was getting famous." He got up from the sofa, went to a desk drawer and pulled out a VHS tape which he popped into a tape player. I was surprised. Very few of us have VHS tapes anymore. The tape brightened and there on a screen was an angelic toddler with blonde hair and blue eyes. Sara.

"Start with the eyelash curler," a voice off-camera coaxed. The child took a wicked looking weapon and held it up to the camera and then applied it to her eye. It looked like a torture device and I wondered how she avoided putting her eye out.

"You have to use the curler first, before you put on the shadow," the toddler was saying. She put the curler down on the floor with an audible clink and held up a palette of pressed colors. "Now this is the fun part."

"Tell them the brand, honey," came the off-screen voice.

"This is from…" the child hesitated, looked off screen.

"Target," came the voice.

"You get it at Target and it's got all kinds of colors." The child picked up a brush. "You have to use one of these special brushes…"

"A number twenty- three brush,"

"Number- twenty- three," she echoed. She dipped the brush into the palette and applied the color to an eyelid. "You can use lots of colors if you want." She dipped the brush again and put a different color on her other lid.

"Well," Ralph said, turning off the video. "That was the beginning. My wife thought it would be fun for her, and it was. The kids who watched YouTube liked her, and she began to get fan mail. By the time she was eleven, we had the big cosmetics companies sending us samples so she could use them on her shows."

Thank God I never had children, I thought. Would I have allowed my daughter to demonstrate makeup as a toddler?

"Sara was always very independent. Even at three, she knew what she wanted and went after it. You never wanted to stand in her way."

"What was it she wanted?"

"To be famous. To be rich. By the time she was eleven, we were doing pretty well from the cosmetics companies. I think Sarah had this idea that one day she would go to Hollywood."

If she had intended to go to Hollywood, why had she headed toward northern New York?

"After she disappeared, the police came and took her computer. They said they were going to try and find out if she was seeing some guy on the internet. I don't think they found anything."

"Did she have any local boyfriends? She was sixteen? Seventeen?"

"Sixteen. No one special. The police interviewed all them boys too. They didn't say anything to me, but I don't think they nailed anyone."

Jud and I were quiet, thinking.

"We had a big fight before she left," Ralph said. "Sara said she wanted more from life than makeup, but I thought makeup would give her a head start on the model business, and of course…" he waved an arm toward the pile of boxes. "we still had some money from the Molly Bee gig, which I thought she shouldn't give up. We'd fought before, so when she didn't come back that night I thought, she's old enough to find her way in the world. She'll come back when she's ready."

He put his head down and for a moment I thought he'd started to cry, but when he lifted his head his eyes were dry.

"Let me show you the studio," he said, rising. We followed him back to the hallway and up the stairs to a bedroom. On the door was a large, colorful sign that said "Molly Bee" decorated with honey bees. He opened the door.

Compared to the sad neglect of the house, the bedroom was palatial. The walls were a pale pink with a hand-painted strip of roses near the ceiling. In the middle of the room was an enormous canopied bed with a spread and pillows in shades of pink, and against one wall was a dressing table with a large studio lamp beside it.

"When she turned six we hired a photographer named Michael Dunster who'd worked with a lot of girls. It cost us a little, but by then people were watching her and we were making money from the sales of cosmetics that the companies sent us. You wouldn't believe it, but makeup for six year olds is big business. I wondered why these kids weren't out playing, but Emily, my wife, thought it would be a gas to see Sara in lipstick and eyeliner. She never wore the stuff outside the house, but by thirteen or fourteen some girls are already wearing makeup to school. Our school didn't let them do it, but I guess some schools do."

Where were the parents in all of this? I wondered.

"We started a business on e-Bay, selling the extra makeup," Ralph said. "We did pretty well. But then Sara started to age out of the business. She was cute when she was six, and perky and fun when she was eleven. But girls who are twelve, want a twelve-year-old showing them how to put on the stuff, not a thirteen or fourteen- year old."

"Couldn't she sell makeup to thirteen and fourteen-year olds?"

"She could. She tried, but there's a lot more competition in that age group. Let me show you."

We went back downstairs and Ralph popped another VHS tape into the player. The girl on the screen was an older version of the toddler in the first video, and a younger version of the dead girl. She was now more professional in the way she held the makeup before applying it, but there was something in her face that looked too world-weary for a thirteen-year old. She was no longer a child. She was a salesman.

"Kids who are fourteen and fifteen can hire a professional photographer and publicist. The field is more crowded and cutthroat. And she wasn't having any fun. She started talking about being a movie star and moving to California, or doing makeup in New York. I mean she was OK in the brains department, but my daughter would never do anything more than be a model or sell makeup."

Poor Sara, I thought. I looked around the run-down house. If I were a teenager growing up here, I would make tracks for the big city too. Only the Adirondacks weren't the big city. What had happened to lure Sara away from her dream?

Chapter Twenty

After our meeting with Ralph, Jud and I discussed trying to find some of Sara's friends in Scranton, but it was already late in the afternoon and I was tired. The next day was Sunday, a day when we would have to make the long trip back to northern New York.

When I got home on Sunday, I took Lilli for an abbreviated version of our usual evening stroll. I was tired. She was tired. On the answering machine was a message from Matt saying that he'd missed me on Saturday and to call him. I needed to do that and to give him an explanation of what I'd been doing. On the other hand, this relationship was brand new. Did I really want to spoil everything before it had even had a chance to flower?

On Monday morning having a little time to myself, I decided to try to phone Celestina. Since her call two weeks ago, I'd seen nothing about a missing person in the newspaper. The phone call went to voicemail. I'd forgotten the daughter's number, so I couldn't call there. I could only hope that the two of them had decided to take a long vacation elsewhere.

I went to my computer and Googled "Molly Bee" and one of the videos Ralph Kyzinski had shown us came up on the screen. If the police had talked to Ralph, they'd seen the tapes and had probably spent a lot of time chatting up Sara's friends. But Sara hadn't been killed in Scranton, she'd been killed here in the Adirondacks. Had her killer been a boyfriend from home, someone she'd dumped and who held a grudge? Someone who'd followed her up here to kill her? Or had her killer been a local? I should have left all this alone, but I needed to know.

Since I didn't have to teach until three, I took out the phone book and looked up beauty salons. Saranac Lake had only one and if Sara had been working in the village, she would have been employed there. It was possible she'd been employed further afield, in Lake Placid or Tupper Lake, but I would start at home.

The hairdressing salon, A Cut Above was in the back of a private home, on a side street. When I walked in, a woman who I guessed was the owner was sitting in one of the chairs reading a *People* magazine. She leaped up as soon as she saw me.

"Do you take walk- ins?"

Of course she did. I was the only one in the place. "You're looking for a cut, or a cut and curl?" she asked looking at me closely. "I could even do some highlights around your face."

I normally wear my hair shoulder-length, but in the months I'd been here in the Adirondacks, I'd let it grow too long. I didn't have time to fuss with my hair, and I had no place to go that required an elaborate do, so short and easy-to-care-for would do the trick.

I slid into a chair and she wrapped a plastic drape around my neck." How much would you like cut off?"

I took a strand of hair and pinched off almost two inches.

"That much?"

"I just can't be bothered with it any more," I said.

"Sure," she said. "And then I'll style it for you."

She turned the chair around and began washing my hair. I always feel pampered when I get my hair done. I can wash it myself but I can't style it, and when I was living in New York I used to get it done about once a month. Even if Scott and I were only going to hang out at home, getting my hair done made me feel festive.

"I'm going to this big event next Saturday," I told the hairdresser, whose name tag identified her as Lorraine. "I'd like to get makeup done. Just to look nice. You don't have anyone here who does that sort of thing, do you?"

"Do you know the girl they found dead in the woods? Sara? She was my makeup person. On Saturday, especially if there were a dance somewhere, all the chairs would be filled with girls just waiting to be made up. I really miss her."

"Did she live here in town?"

"I don't know where she lived. If I had to reach her, I would have to call her cell. It was very frustrating, because sometimes I had girls waiting here and no way to reach her. I told her that if she gave me her address, I would drive out to her house and pick her up, but she still wouldn't tell me where she lived."

"Did she have parents, boyfriends, or girlfriends?"

"Just the Boxer boy, he hung around here sometimes waiting for her to be finished. Sometimes he brought his little sister. I feel sorry for Darryl. His father was arrested for cooking meth, and his mother is an alcoholic. They are barely scraping by. Even so, I told him that when Sara was here, he and his sister had to hang out elsewhere."

My hair had been washed and Lorraine had started the cut. "I suppose you know a lot of the kids around here," I said.

"Sure do. The bright ones head out of town as soon as they graduate. Unless you want to work in a restaurant or a motel, or take folks out fishing in the summer, there isn't much. Saranac Lake is better than some places because we got retirees moving up here. Retirees don't have kids in the schools and they pay taxes, but you know, from November to April things are pretty slow, and then the retirees might go south for the winter."

"Was doing makeup Sara's only job here?"

"It was the only thing she did for me, but she waitressed at The Glass Frog in Lake Placid and she did makeup for "Be a Model for a Day" in Watertown."

"Be a Model for a Day?"

"The girls come in, get fitted with a pretty dress, get their hair and makeup done and their picture took. Sometimes Mr. Lincoln, sends the name of a girl to an agency in New York City. I don't know if any of these girls ever get to be real models, but it's a fun afternoon. When there's a prom coming up, "Be A Model," runs the event from Thursday to Saturday. After Sara left, I tried to contact their makeup person, but it's too far away for someone to drive here. I really miss the extra money that Sara brought in."

She had curled my hair and was brushing it out. It looked nice, and I felt as pampered as I'd felt all those months ago in New York City. I only wished I had somewhere special to go.

Chapter Twenty-One

I was driving home from my Monday art class when the phone rang. It was Jud. "Call me," he said.

Jud could wait. I needed to get home, walk my dog and feed her, think about what I could nuke for supper and sit. Then, I would call Jud.

"What's up?" I asked when I finally got around to the call. I was in my sloppy sweats, with my half-eaten supper and a glass of juice on the coffee table in front of me. I'd muted the TV which was showing national news.

"You take your time getting back to me," he said.

I almost hung up. I wasn't in the mood to deal with his pissyness.

"Sorry," he said. "I'd like you to take a look at what I've written about Sara Kyzinski. And if you've got anything more to add, tell me. I'm e-mailing you the document now."

I went to my computer and booted it up. The first thing to appear was the portrait of Sara that Ralph had shown us. I don't know how Jud got it; maybe he stole it, or just snapped a shot with his phone. For the first time, people would see a girl who up to now had only been a story in the paper. They would see how pretty she had been and they would imagine the end of her young life. They might also realize, as I was now understanding, that someone in this small community had befriended a stranger, lured her into the woods, wrapped a ligature around her neck and pulled, and while she struggled, snuffed out her life. It's easy for all of us to think of a killer as a stranger. Harder to think of a killer as someone we might meet in the grocery store, or in a restaurant, someone we live near, or see boating on the lake. It is harder to think of someone who lives among us, as someone who would kill.

I read Jud's article which talked about Sara's early history demonstrating makeup on YouTube, and her hopes to have a career in New York City or Hollywood. There was a picture of Sara's bedroom door with the "Molly Bee" sign, and the interior with the frilly bed, the dressing table and the spotlight on a pedestal. Jud had also taken a photo of the boxes piled in the corner of the living room. The last paragraph was about Ralph selling unused makeup on e-Bay, seeming to profit from his daughter's death.

I called Jud back. "It's good," I said. "When will it be in the paper?"

"On Sunday. Do you have anything to add?"

"She was doing makeup at a salon called A Cut Above. The owner thought I was just a customer looking for a cut and curl so it would be awkward if you repeat that."

"What's the owner's name?"

"Lorraine."

"I'll go down and see her. I'll take Sara's picture with me."

We were quiet. "How's your girlfriend doing?" I asked.

"We broke up. It wasn't a great relationship to begin with and I decided we both needed to move on."

He'd used her to get information, and when she was no longer of value, he'd dumped her. Maybe I needed to distance myself from this sleezebag. At that moment someone knocked. "Gotta go, Jud," I said, and went to answer the door.

Matt Waring stood there.

"Can I come in?"

I looked around. There were bras and panties drying on a rack near the window. I had thrown my coat over a chair and there were books and magazines piled in a corner. Lilli's toys were scattered around the floor and Lilli herself got up from where she was sleeping and went over and gave Matt a quiet nudge in the crotch with her nose.

As he reached down to pat her, I rushed toward the chair, scooped up the clothing and folding the rack at the same time, shoved everything into the bedroom.

"I tried to call but your phone was busy," he said.

I waved him to a seat, the only place to sit other than the couch. "Can I get you a drink?" I asked.

He looked at the remnant of my one- bowl macaroni and cheese. "I interrupted your supper," he said.

"Nope," I said, picking up the food in its plastic container and depositing it in the trash. "On the days when I work, it's just easier."

"You don't have to apologize to me. I eat the same bad stuff. If I don't have something I can heat up in three minutes, I go out. It's hard to be single and not gain weight."

I got up and moved to the kitchen. "Did you say beer or wine?" Before he'd even answered, I was pushing bottles around in the refrigerator. Having him in my crappy little apartment was making me nervous.

"You've done something to your hair," he said. "I like it."

"Thanks," I said, handing him a glass of red wine. I didn't even remember what he'd asked for.

"Would you like to go out for a drink? I promise I won't keep you out too late."

"Sure," I said. "That sounds nice." Being in a bar would make me less nervous than having him assess the wreck of my apartment. If it were too noisy to talk, we could just sit and look at each other. I rushed into the bedroom and put on jeans and a nice brightly-colored cashmere sweater, one of the high-priced bits of clothing I'd brought from New York. Some dangling earrings with red stones helped too. I ran my hand over the new hairdo, put on some bright lipstick and I was ready.

We drove to a bar called The Heron's Roost, tucked on a side street. I normally don't drink at bars. They are too noisy for my taste, but this was Monday night at the end of the season, so except for a few men and one or two women holding down seats at the bar, it was quiet.

Matt found us a table in the corner. I ordered a white wine and he got a beer.

"I was sorry you couldn't come on Saturday," he said, when he came back to the table with our drinks.

"You needed someone to hide for the dogs."

He smiled. "That part is never fun, is it? But we take turns. My good friend Kelly was there, so we had a good time.

Kelly? A good friend Kelly? Matt had taken out his cell phone and was scrolling through pictures. He held it up to me. I recognized Matt and Jim, Hershey and WhizBang. Beside Jim was a small woman with silver hair, holding a standard poodle on a leash. All three looked tired and dirty. "Kelly's just a friend," Matt said. "In case you were thinking otherwise."

"I wasn't thinking anything," I lied. He was, I told myself, entitled to have a friendship with a woman. Kelly wasn't bad looking, and he probably had more in common with her than he did with me, because Kelly already had a search and rescue dog, while all I could do for the group was hide. *Grow up, Drew*, I said to myself. *They're just friends. Nothing more.*

"So how was New York City?" he asked. "If that's too nosy, you don't have to tell me."

Why had I said I was going there? I couldn't for the life of me remember.

"You were going to be with a friend?" he prodded.

"She's getting married," I said. "We used to work together and she's getting married and wanted me to help her pick out a dress." I hated lying to Matt but I wasn't sure he would approve of what I'd done.

"When's the wedding?"

"The wedding?"

"Isn't that why you went to New York last weekend? To help your friend pick out a wedding dress? "

"Oh yeah. It's at Christmas. She's going to put me up at her place, since the apartment I used to live in is obviously gone. Of course, it's possible I could stay with my dad who lives in Manhattan." I was blathering, trying to use up conversational space so he wouldn't ask more questions, but he seemed to have his mind on other things, fiddling with his paper napkin, shredding it slowly into small pieces.

"What's wrong?"

"WhizBang has cancer," he said. "Jim's broken up about it."

I leaned forward. "I am so sorry," I said. "I couldn't imagine that happening to Lilli."

"Jim's looking for a pup to train. He's gone back to the same breeder, but there won't be any new babies for a month and then it will be close to the start of winter."

"Do the dogs train year round?"

"Sometimes. We can still use the old paper mill in winter, but going into the woods is tough on the dogs' feet especially if there is crusty snow. Are you still thinking of training Lilli?"

With all that was going on in my life, I hadn't been thinking of Lilli, but it would be nice to spend more time with Matt. "I have been thinking about it," I lied.

"Great. Next Saturday we're going out again. There's a place where they used to make wooden bowls near Tupper Lake. It's a two story building that's in pretty good shape. The owners don't mind our using it."

"Sure," I said. "Saturday would be nice."

"One more thing," Matt said. "There's a dance at the Hilton on Saturday night. A fundraiser for the search and rescue people. Would you like to come?"

"With you?"

"Well, of course."

I would need a dress. When I was with Scott, we never went out so I had nothing in the way of dresses. I would have to see what I could find.

"I'd love to," I said.

For the next half hour, I talked about my teaching job. Matt told me about growing up in the Adirondacks, about his father who was a local lawyer who'd never made much money but loved the area, and his mother who had been a gardener, canner, quilter, singer in the local choir and, from what it sounded like, saint. At ten o'clock we headed back to the apartment. Matt walked me to the door of the apartment.

"I had a good time tonight, Drew," he said.

"Me too."

"I'll see you on Saturday morning. Dress like you did the last time."

"And bring Lilli."

"Of course."

He reached forward and kissed me. I moved into his kiss, feeling his arms warm around me, his lips pressed against mine. His body was pressed against mine too and I could feel his arousal. Was it too soon to ask him up? Maybe, but he was so nice, so warm and inviting.

He pulled away. "Gotta go," he said.

I could have asked you in, I thought.

Chapter Twenty-Two

When I got back to the apartment I couldn't sleep. I should have been spending some time working on my art class for tomorrow. Instead I booted up my computer and Googled "Be A Model" and was led to a website that featured teenage girls dressed in sparkly dresses, lavishly made up with their hair newly coiffed. The website said that the next session would be this coming weekend and they were taking reservations now. A phone number was given and I copied it down. If I were in Watertown on Friday, I might be able to pick up a dress there.

On Tuesday afternoon, after my class, I drove to Lake Placid and The Glass Frog, where Sara Kyzinski had been waitressing two days a week. The 'Frog' was a largish building on Main Street with windows looking right out onto Mirror Lake. The hours listed on the website were three to ten, and having worked in restaurants in my youth, I hoped just before the supper hour would not be too disruptive to the staff. But this was Tuesday, generally a quiet evening for restaurants. I had taken Lilli with me, hoping for a quick walk, but when I got to the restaurant, I left her in the car, and headed toward the entrance.

I was met at the door by a server. It was now about four.

"Are you looking for a meal, Ma'am?" he asked. "We're just setting up for dinner."

"Could I speak to the manager?"

He looked startled. Did he think I was going to complain about the service? "There is nothing wrong with the restaurant," I said. "I just wanted a word with him."

"With her, you mean. You want the owner Tedra Allen. I'll get her."

In a few minutes a woman about my own age approached. She was slender with frosted blonde hair and small features.

"Can I help you?"

"I wonder if we could talk about Sara Kyzinski. I understand that she worked here?"

Tedra nodded and I could see sadness cross her face. "She was a great kid. I'm sure her parents must be devastated."

"Do you have some time now?" I asked, looking around. A man was setting up one table and a young woman was putting a clean cloth on another

"I can give you ten minutes," Tedra said. She waived over one of the servers. "Could you get us two cups of coffee, Larry?"

She looked at me. "Why are you interested in Sara?"

"It's a long story. This past summer I was caught in the woods when the microburst came through, and got lost."

"That's right. You were there for a while. I read about you in the paper. It's lucky they found you."

"When I was in the woods, I saw an image of a girl, a ghost. When I got out, I convinced the police to go looking for her. It was Sara. I was there when she was found."

"How awful for you."

"It was. I felt as though she wanted me to find her. And now I just can't let her fade into the background."

"I don't think the police will let her fade into the background." She took a sip of the coffee that had just been delivered. "I can't tell you very much about her. She came looking for a job here about the second week in June. The thirteenth I think." She took another sip, staring through the window at the lighted houses that ringed the lake. "I inherited this restaurant from my father who wanted to move to Florida, but when he left I wanted to keep all his employees because I know what it's like to support yourself year round here. But that meant when Sara came looking I had no job for her."

"A week later one of my regulars quit, so I gave her Thursday and Friday evenings. She was a good kid who worked hard. The only problem I had was that she flirted with the cooks and the waiters. It was nothing serious on her part, but it made things unsettled. She drove a beat-up red Volvo with Pennsylvania plates, so I assumed she had come from there."

"You don't know where she lived? Up here, I mean."

"Somewhere near Saranac Lake. That's what she said."

"Did she ever tell you the reason she'd come here?"

"She said she had a fight with her father and I wondered if he knew she was here. If I had a daughter Sara's age, I wouldn't have been happy about her working so far from home. But I try not to pry into my employee's lives."

I couldn't think of a single other question to ask Tedra. I thanked her for the coffee and moved toward the door.

"I hope they find the person who killed her," Tedra said. "She was a great kid."

I thanked Tedra for her time and went back out to the car. Then Lilli and I took our walk.

On Wednesday I had my last art class of the week and for the third day in a row, Darryl Boxer was absent. Given his chaotic home life, it might be business as usual for him to skip school, but we needed to talk, and I had no idea where he lived. As the class moved to its close, and the students started to file out, I stopped a girl who I'd seen talking to him.

"Janelle," I said.

"Yeah?"

"Darryl hasn't been in class for three days. Is he sick?"

She shrugged. "He skips class a lot. I don't think he cares too much about graduating. He says that once he's famous, no one will ask where he went to high school."

"I need to talk with him. Do you know where he lives?"

"Outside of town. It's a run-down trailer park called Garden Acres."

"You don't know the number?"

"You can't miss his place. The trailer is bright green. Darryl's dad painted it one night when he was stoned. And there's a dog tied up behind. A Rottweiler. Be careful of him"

A bright green, badly-painted trailer with a vicious dog. Easy to find.

As I was driving to the trailer park, I thought more about Darryl. He seemed to know a lot about Sara and I'm sure the police had tried to question him. Maybe because of Darryl's distrust of the law, he'd refused to talk. I needed to learn what had drawn Sara Kyzinski from Pennsylvania, to the Adirondacks and Darryl seemed to be the key to that.

There was no garden at Garden Acres, only a crowded collection of rusting trailers, most of them with additions like wooden porches, dying plants in pots, junk cars, discarded children's toys, broken chairs and empty liquor bottles. All these things were scattered around the perimeter of the dwellings, a sure sign that the down-and-out lived here. I found the bright green trailer, stepped up to the front door and knocked. Immediately a large, black dog shot toward me from around the corner. I leaped away from the door, sure that I was going to be mauled. The dog jerked to the end of his leash, snapping and growling. Cautiously, keeping as far away as I could, I made my way toward the door again.

"Darryl," I called. "It's Drew Morgan from the art class. Can I talk to you?"

I waited. Maybe he was asleep, or stoned, or drunk. Maybe he had another dog inside, a twin to the monster still baring his teeth at me, and I would be savaged as soon as I set foot inside.

"Darryl," I called again. I waited and had just decided to turn around and go home when the door opened. Darryl Boxer stood there, wearing a dirty T-shirt and jeans. He looked like he'd just woken up.

"Can we talk?"

He moved aside and I stepped up into the stale funk of a trailer about the size of my apartment. A faded couch with threadbare arms sat under one window and opposite it, a Formica table, worn to white stood beside a tiny sink, stove and refrigerator. The table was decorated with a variety of cigarette burns and held an unlit joint in an ashtray beside a can of beer. Darryl sat down opposite me and took a swig of the beer.

"You talked to your father?"

I'd sent my father some pictures by e-mail and though my dad had said Darryl had talent, he hadn't actually promised him anything.

"I'm getting out of here next week," he said. "Give me your dad's address and I'll pop in to see him."

"You're better off going to his gallery," I said. My father is a very private man. Even his most ardent buyers never went to his home.

"Let me give you the name of his gallery," I said. "You can visit him there, and get a look at the type of art he sells."

"You can't give me his home address?" Darryl whined. "You're just playing me aren't you? Telling me how great my stuff is, when all the time you know it's crap."

"It isn't crap," I said with some force. "You have talent, but it takes a while to become known as an artist. Believe me, I've been painting for quite a while, and I still don't sell much."

"Maybe you just ain't that good," he said.

Had we reached an impasse? Darryl tossed the empty beer can in a basket and went to the refrigerator for another.

"You knew Sara Kyzinski before she came up here, didn't you?" I said.

I don't think it was the question he was expecting. He nodded.

"Did she come here to the Adirondacks because of you, Darryl?"

Another small nod. This wasn't going to be easy.

"Tell me about you and Sara."

He shrugged. I waited.

"You didn't tell Detective Weims about your relationship, did you?"

"Why the hell should I talk to him? The cops ain't ever done nothin good for me. Screw them." He looked at me slyly. "You gonna tell em what I said?"

I shook my head. I was taking a chance just being here, but I needed to know the whole story.

"You gonna get me in to see your dad?" he asked.

I sighed. "I will do my best," I said. "So tell me how you met Sara."

"One of those internet dating sites. I was just fooling around. The girls around here are all dogs or ho's. I wanted to hook up with someone new."

Someone who didn't know your father ran a Meth lab, and your mother was an alcoholic. I had an idea how cruel kids can be to each other.

"She advertised herself as an artist, so I thought, that's cool, we can talk art. When she said she was into makeup, I almost ditched her, but she was good looking, and smart. We got to know each other a bit on the internet. She was trying to get out of Pennsylvania 'cause she was fighting with her dad a lot, so I sent her some money to buy an old car. When she drove up here, I'd already found a place for her to stay."

"You found a place for her to live? Where was it?"

"It was great. No one would ever find her there."

"Why was that?"

"It's out in the woods, and folks don't want to go near it, 'cause of the murder?"

"What murder?"

"You live on another planet lady? *The* murder. The doctor that was shot a few years ago. His name was LeBrun. Lived way out in the woods."

"I've only been here for a few months. I've never heard of this murder."

"It was in all the papers. Anyway, I went to the cabin, straightened it up, got the water working, though I couldn't do nothing about the lights. I thought it would be just the two of us, private-like, but then she had to bring her sister with her."

Lorraine at A Cut Above had said the girl was *Darryl's* sister.

"And then, after all I'd done to find her a place to live and sending her money to buy a car, she wouldn't let me come in the cabin. We started fighting a lot. I was sorry I'd asked her to come."

"What were you fighting about?"

"Lots of things. Mostly the fact that she wanted to move to New York City where she could make real money. She said I had deceived her, told her I would help her and I hadn't done a thing. I said I'd found her the house, hadn't I? But it wasn't enough."

"So you broke up?"

"Not right away. She was so fine I didn't want to give her up, but by then she was going out with this other dude who was giving her presents, taking her out to nice places. I couldn't compete with that."

"Did you know who this other man was?"

"Nope. But he was buying her lots of expensive stuff. Nothin I could afford."

"When did she tell you she was leaving the Adirondacks?"

"Almost from the first she talked about it. Saranac Lake was a dump, we were all retards, and nobody with any brains would live in a trailer park like mine. I know what this place looks like, but there are good people here. All she wanted was to get to the city. After we stopped going out, I drove by The Glass Frog after her shift was over, just to see her, but the lady told me Sara hadn't showed up for work. I figured she'd finally saved enough to get away."

He had finished. He leaned back in the chair and took a swig from the can of beer.

"You should go back to school, Darryl," I said. "If you don't have an education, no one will ever hire you."

"Once your father sees my art, he's gonna shit himself trying to sign me up," Darryl said. He rose from the seat and went into a bedroom and came back with a watercolor pad which he spread out on the table. The paintings were good, but not great. It is possible for a relative unknown to make it in the art world, but it is also very rare. The artist has to have something special, something unusual, something that would make him memorable once the viewer has left the gallery. Darryl was good, but he had none of those qualities.

I stood. "Thank you for your time," I said. Darryl nodded. He pushed the pad of paintings into my hand. "Give him this," he said. "Wait," he said snatching back the pad and scribbling a phone number on the front. "Tell him he can call me any time."

When I exited the trailer, the Rottweiler was nowhere to be seen. Nevertheless, I double-timed my walk to the car and got inside as soon as I could. Sitting in my car I looked back at the badly painted bright green trailer. Darryl had loved Sara and Sara had betrayed him. Could he have killed her? I imagined the scenario. She comes to the trailer, knocks on the door and he steps outside to talk. She tells him this place is a dump, that he's never helped her and that she's driving to New York City the next day. He pushes her against the trailer, starts choking her and when she falls to the ground the Rottweiler comes roaring out from behind the trailer and starts biting her leg. Darryl finds a wire and continues to choke until Sara lies dead on the ground.

Could it have happened this way? I suppose so. The place where Sara's body had been dumped was accessible to anyone, and was well known as a place where teens hung out. If Darryl had killed Sara and then cut off her foot to hide the dog bites, where had he put Sara's red Volvo? Darryl might have hidden it behind the trailer where, because of the vicious Rottweiler, no one would look. All of this was possible, but I couldn't keep these things to myself any longer. I needed to talk to a detective.

Chapter Twenty-Three

The next day was Thursday. I had my work at the motel from eight- thirty until three-thirty which would give me time to go looking for Sara's cabin. I called Jud.

"Whatcha got?"

"I got a clue to where Sara was living," I said. "Do you know anything about a murder that happened in Saranac Lake a few years ago?"

"Sure. Sandy LeBrun. He was a local doctor, living in a cabin in the woods when he was shot."

"Do you know *where* he was living Jud?"

"Yeah. I think I can find it. Is that where Sara was?"

"My student Darryl Boxer helped her move in."

"Pretty clever. That place has been empty for a few years. No one wants to go near it."

"I won't be off work until three-thirty. Can I meet you somewhere?"

"Come to the newspaper. You can park in the lot and I'll drive you."

"Promise you won't go there without me."

He sighed. "What the hell," he said. "OK."

At quarter to four, I was parked in the parking lot. I waited for fifteen minutes before I saw Jud's porky figure exiting the front door of the building. He tapped on the door to the car and I opened it. "My vehicle," he said.

"You don't like my car, do you?" I said when I was sitting beside him. "What's wrong with it?"

"It smells like dog and it makes me sneeze."

"Well, I hate your taste in music, so I guess we're even."

He had started to drive away, and we were almost out of the village itself when he stopped at a break in the trees at the side of the road.

"And this guy was a doctor? Must have liked his privacy."

"LeBrun was some fancy plastic surgeon in New York City when he and his wife moved to Euclid, north of here. Then his little boy was killed. No one knew who did it, but LeBrun was busted up, moved here to the Adirondacks and bought this little cabin so he could live quietly. He worked a couple of days a week at a local clinic."

"Who killed him?"

"I don't remember. It was all solved up north. You should ask Jim Weims ; he was the detective who ran the case down here."

I looked carefully at the break in the trees, where there was indeed a road, but badly overgrown. It was starting to get dark, and cold; I was still in my maid's uniform with only a sweater to protect me from the chill. I wish I'd brought my coat. Jud looked at my shoes, the ones I wear cleaning rooms.

"It might be muddy," he said. "I hope you're prepared."

"How far is the house?"

"Almost half a mile." He took out a flashlight and shone it on the road.

"Half a mile? Damn."

I took out a flashlight of my own. It was small and underpowered, one I used mainly to find my way to my seat in a darkened movie theatre, or move down the sidewalk late at night. In the growing dark, the trees encroached menacingly, and I thought of animals waiting. The anxiety that I'd felt when I was lost and forced to sleep alone in the woods came roaring back and I started to tremble.

"I need to go back," I said. "Ever since I was lost, I can't…"

"Yes you can, Drew. We're in this together." He put his arm through mine. I have no romantic interest in Jud Weinstein, but at that moment, his bulky presence was reassuring.

"What made you want to be a painter?" he asked, making conversation to take my mind off the scariness of our surroundings.

"My dad is well-known. By the time I was born, he already had major shows in lots of the big galleries in the city."

"Good for him."

"Yeah. He had the knack of painting the kind of stuff people want in their living rooms, huge realistic images of nature, mountains, oceans, sometimes animals. He had a studio in our apartment and when I was a kid, I would go up and paint with him."

"So, you were going to follow in his footsteps?"

155

"No. I was going to be a veterinarian. My best pal in the world, besides my sister, was a rescued Malamute named Big Bruce. But he died..."

"And then you decided to paint?"

"No, my sister died and my life went to hell."

We walked on in silence. Silence is not healthy. It draws me back down into the darkness of those days, a place that I have tried hard to stay away from, but which, like stepping into a fast stream, sweeps you along without your permission.

Living up to our expectations, the road was muddy and rutted, and the trees, given time to grow without restraints, now rudely encroached, leaving no room to pass. Additionally, it was getting colder, and I wished I'd worn more than a light sweater. But walking was better than standing still because I could be marginally warmer. Once or twice, I saw eyes peering at us from the underbrush. Deer, raccoons, skunks, coyotes? I knew that none of those animals attacked, but I wished fiercely that I were home with my dog, slouched on the couch with a good book and a glass of wine.

At last, we reached a widening of the road and were looking at a small cabin beyond which was a pond, silvered in the dying light. I followed Jud as he stepped up onto the porch that had a pile of firewood on one end and two rocking chairs on the other. Pushing open the door, we walked inside.

We stepped into a large living room with a wood stove on one side with two upholstered chairs facing it. On one of the chairs was a copy of *Teen* magazine. Against another wall was a door and a small wooden table with chairs. A kerosene lantern stood on the table. Jud moved to the mantle above the fireplace and, finding matches, lit the lantern, which gave the room a cozy glow. We could look out the front window to the pond, where a smear of yellow light below the ebony sky was reflected in the water. It was a lovely view, one I tried to use to pull my thoughts away from the dread of hiking out of the woods in the dark.

"Come on," I said. "Let's see what's here." The kitchen was small, with a tiny propane refrigerator, propane stove and a sink. There was a dishpan in the sink, clean dishes in the strainer, and dishwashing soap and cloth towels beside it. Opening the cupboards, we found rice and cereal in mouse- proof containers. For a girl who'd only recently come from the city, Sara knew how to live in the woods. But then maybe Darryl had set all this up for her. We went back to the living room and opened the door to what was an empty bedroom. The bed was just a bare mattress, but in the cupboard was a neat pile of sheets and blankets with a pillow on top. There was nothing in the tiny dresser that gave any clue to the occupant. On the single chair was a teddy bear.

The second bedroom, which must have been Sara's was a gold mine of information. The bed was made with clean sheets and what appeared to be a new comforter. On a dressing table were many kinds of makeup and in a pile in a corner, jewelry.

"Did you see this, Jud?" I asked. I held up a pearl necklace. "This looks expensive. How can someone who is waiting tables and working in a beauty parlor afford this stuff?" Jud had whipped out a camera, a huge heavy deal that he'd lugged all the way from the road, and was snapping pictures. I drifted toward the closet where there were evening dresses and hanging beside the dresses, a cashmere sweater, leather pants, silk blouses, even a fur jacket. I showed them to Jud and he began taking pictures.

I took the fur jacket and held it up. "What do you think? Sugar Daddy? Darryl said almost as much."

"So where's her purse?" Jud asked. "And her cell phone? No woman goes off without those."

I had started to open a drawer on one side of the dressing table, but something stiff was caught inside, making it hard to pull. "Bring your flashlight over here, Jud, will you?" I asked.

I pushed my hand into the drawer and mashed down the paper. Then I pulled the drawer open. The stiff paper turned out to be a series of photographs.

"Holy cow," Jud said.

There, in color, were three nude photographs of Sara. In the first she was on her knees, facing the camera, her naked breasts hanging down. She was wearing a diamond necklace and you could clearly see the pubic triangle between her legs. In the second photo she was wearing the same necklace, but she was on her back, her butt on the floor, her breasts thrust forward, supporting herself on her bent elbows. In the third, she was on her butt again, and you were looking at her face and breasts through her upraised legs. Her only jewelry was the necklace.

"These were professionally taken," Jud said. "This isn't some teen with a cell phone sexting his friends."

"You think she was paid?"

"Could be." He was back to snapping pictures. I took my own picture of the Sara nudes before Jud tucked them into his pocket.

"We should be getting back," I said.

"Afraid of the dark?" Jud asked.

I didn't want to admit that I had been dreading the walk back, so I looked around the room, trying to think what we might have missed. "We have to tell the police about this," I said.

Jud had moved back into the living room to get long shots and close ups.

"You know once the cops see this, we won't be able to return," I continued.

He didn't answer. I went back to the bedroom, thinking about the girl who had lived here. When I'd first begun to know Sara and understood how she supported herself in a place where she was a stranger, I admired her grit. Now, I wasn't so sure. Certainly she needed to live, but wasn't there a better way to earn money than soft porn?

Come on, Drew, I thought. *You weren't in her shoes. You don't know what she was working to get away from. Getting your picture taken, doesn't mean you're having sex with someone.*

I was just about to leave the room when I noticed something. A tiny sliver of pink just under the mattress of the bed. I went closer and looked at it. It was the edge of a cell phone. Sara's phone.

Pulling it out, I tucked it into the pocket of my sweater. This was not going to be scrutinized by anyone until I'd seen it myself.

Jud was in the kitchen, still snapping pictures. I went into the bathroom, a place barely large enough to turn around in. The medicine cabinet over the sink was empty, but there was a tube of toothpaste and a toothbrush sitting next to a glass on the tiny counter. The towels were clean. The toilet and shower were clean and, except for some dust on the floor, the place looked as though someone had just stepped out. I went back into the living room and looked into the wood stove. There were ashes inside and some half burned wood. Clearly someone had used it.

"Ready?" Jud said from the door. He had his flashlight out and lit.

"I'm ready," I said.

Later, back in my apartment, I changed out of my uniform which had been smeared with debris from encroaching plants. I had one more day of work this week and no time to launder it. Maybe a good brushing would have to do.

After I'd changed into my sweats, let Lilli out to do her business, and then got back in and poured myself a glass of wine, I looked at the cell phone. I tried to turn it on but the battery was dead. Leaving the phone charging from the computer, I rolled into bed.

Chapter Twenty-Four

The next day was Friday. I would work my eight to three shift at the motel, and then drive to Watertown to talk to people at "Model for a Day." This time, instead of keeping my uniform on when I left work, I changed into a blouse and jeans, spritzed myself with a little cologne to cover the smell of ancient motel rooms and headed out.

By calling ahead, I'd made sure that "Be a Model for a Day" was still going on, and because it was about a two-hour ride, I was sure things would still be going strong at five. When I got to the mall, I didn't need to worry about finding the event because a long line of teen age girls, some of them carrying dresses, some with suitcases were slowly moving toward a storefront. A thin woman wearing a tight black dress and a weary look was working the line, trying to sort out those who needed a hair do and makeup from those who only needed makeup or only wanted a dress.

"Ma'am," I said, stepping out of line. "Can we talk?"

"Who are you?" she snapped.

"A reporter from *The Mountain Journal*. I was hoping to do a story on this event."

"You should have talked to me first," she barked. "I do not have any time to sit down with anyone."

"What if I work with you?"

"Can you do makeup?"

I shook my head.

"Hair?"

I shook my head.

"Help a girl get into a dress?"

I nodded.

"You'll do" she said grabbing me by the arm and pulling me forward.

"What's your name?"

"Drew Morgan."

"I'm Mary Grinnell." We had reached a pair of rooms that had been purposed for the event. Against one wall of the first room were three chairs that had been set up for hairdressers who were at the moment washing, curling and blow drying hair. Against the other wall of the same room, a middle- aged woman was applying makeup. Mary led me to the second room where a rack of dresses sat beside a makeshift nylon dressing area, and a man was shooting photos of girls against a cloth screen. A tall man with grey hair, who I guessed was a supervisor, was walking around.

"Here's the deal," Mary said. "We get these dresses donated, so anyone without a prom dress can buy one for a dollar. Some of the girls come with their mothers, and some with their friends, but lots of them need help choosing a dress and then putting it on in the dressing room. If you can do that, it would help a lot."

"Sure," I said.

She looked at me closely for the first time. "I'm sorry I was short with you. We get people who promise to volunteer and never show up. Can I get you a coffee?"

"Thanks. That would be nice."

My first customer was a thirteen- year- old girl, who was all alone and choosing a dress for her first prom. I helped her pick three then I went into the dressing room with her and we tried them on. She was young and thin and very excited about going to her first dance. Had I ever been this way? Of course.

As I watched her admire herself in the mirror, I thought of the first dance Carley and I had gone to together. Double dating. Carley had worn a mint-green off the shoulder dress, and I, the elder sister wore pale pink with a low cut bodice. That had been the year I was sixteen, Carley fourteen. The next year my sister would be dead.

"I like this one the best," the girl was saying. "What's the matter?" She was looking at me. "You look awfully sad."

"I was remembering a dance my sister and I went to when she was just about your age."

The girl shrugged. After some discussion, she chose the dress she was wearing and I directed her to the line for makeup and hair.

The next girl was a bit older and had obviously done this before. When we got into the dressing room with her choices, she said "You're new."

I nodded.

"It's better to have a woman here," she said. "Sometimes, when we're in here alone, Mr. Lincoln will burst in. He does it on purpose just to catch us naked."

"Who's Mr. Lincoln?"

"You don't know George Lincoln? He's the tall guy you've seen walking around. They let him do what he wants because he's the one who raises the money, but I don't like him. He's creepy."

"He comes into the dressing rooms when the girls are trying on gowns?"

"More than that. He pretends to admire us when we're having our picture took, runs his hands over our breasts and bums. I tried to slap him once and was told not to. You don't mess with Mr. Lincoln."

She had put on the dress and I helped her zip it up the back. "Did you ever have your makeup done by a girl named Sara Kyzinski?"

The girl turned in front of the mirror. "I'm not sure," she said, admiring herself in the dress. "I think I like the blue one better." I helped her unzip the dress and she stepped out of it. "Sara? Yeah. She was here earlier. Long blonde hair, blue eyes. She could have been a model. I told her that."

"Did you ever talk with her while she was doing your makeup?"

The girl had stepped into the blue dress, which did suit her better. I zipped up the back and she turned before the mirror. "Wait a minute. Oh my God. Was she the one they found dead?

She told me she was trying to get enough money to move away. I remember that now. We aren't supposed to pay anyone, but I gave her a nice tip."

She admired herself for a few minutes more and then said, "I think this is the dress I'm getting."

I unzipped her, and we carried the dresses out together. When she was about to leave, the girl turned and said, "I liked Sara. She was a nice kid. I feel really bad about what happened."

After two hours of helping girls try on dresses, I needed a cup of coffee and a pee, not necessarily in that order, and since the line had shortened considerably, I wandered into the next room to find Mary. I told her what I needed and she said she'd walk with me to the Food Court.

We headed out into the mall. Friday night generates a lot of traffic, especially from Fort Drum, and shopping, or just looking, is an inexpensive form of entertainment for young military families. Mary and I walked, without talking, to the ladies' room and when I had used the facilities and washed my hands we headed back.

"Coffee?" Mary asked, when we neared a kiosk.

"Sure," I said. Mary pulled out her wallet and bought two cups. "Would you like a muffin?"

I nodded. This would be my supper. But instead of heading back toward "Be a Model," Mary plunked herself onto a bench.

"I've been here since four- thirty," Mary said. "This is the first chance I've had to sit." It was now eight-thirty, and according to the website, 'Be a Model' would only be open for half an hour more.

"Will you be here tomorrow?"

"All day." She leaned toward me. "I couldn't convince you to come in again, could I?"

"Sorry," I said. She sipped her coffee, and I could see from the shadows under her eyes how tired she was.

"Tell me about George Lincoln," I said.

"George? He started this whole thing. He convinced the bridal stores to donate the dresses, got a beauty salon to provide the hairdressers that he pays for, and gets us the makeup girl and photographer. We couldn't do this without him."

"One of the girls said he comes into the dressing rooms when the girls are changing."

"He does?" she said, but I could see it wasn't a surprise.

"And you let him do this?"

"We don't let him do anything. George is the king around here. I know he takes liberties with these girls, and most of them are too young or too shy to say anything. Once in a while we get a complaint from a parent, but you know men will be men."

"I don't think all men are like that," I said. "At least the ones I know aren't. How does a girl feel when a middle-aged man bursts in on her when she's dressing, or runs his hands over her when she's having her picture taken? I thought the purpose of this event was to raise a girl's self esteem. What kind of mixed message are you sending when you let things like that happen?"

Mary looked at me. "What's your name?"

I thought I'd already told her. "Drew," I said.

"Drew, I don't know how long you've lived in this area, but many of these girls come from families where, in spite of the fact that both parents are working, they still live below the poverty line. This program gives girls a night when they can wear a beautiful gown, and when their hair and face are perfect. It is a night they will probably remember for the rest of their lives. If I told George Lincoln that he could no longer be part of this event, we wouldn't *have* an event. I know how he treats the girls; it's not something I like, but having George here is the price we pay to help a lot of girls."

She drained her coffee, tossed the cup in the trash and we headed back toward the storefront. By now, there were only a few girls on the makeup/hairdressing side. I walked to the other room, where a lone girl was standing beside the rack of dresses trying to choose. Behind the curtain of the makeshift dressing room, I saw a girl's bare feet and a pair of dark shoes. I pulled open the curtain.

The tall, grey haired man I'd seen earlier was standing with his back to me and hunched up against the wall of the dressing room, facing him was a girl of about thirteen, trying to hide her naked breasts.

"What are you doing here?" I asked.

He turned and glared at me. In spite of the expensive suit, he was not an attractive man.

"Do you know who I am?" he asked.

167

"I think I do," I said. "But that does not give you the right to be here. You could be the President of the United States, and this dressing room is still off limits to men."

"You are fired."

"Go ahead. I'm a volunteer."

"What's your name?"

"Drew Morgan."

"You will be very sorry you spoke to me this way, Drew Morgan," he said and stormed out.

The girl huddled against the wall had started to cry. I moved toward her and took her in my arms. "I am so sorry, honey," I said. "I will be here from now on, and if he tries to get in again he'll have to step over my dead body."

My words brought a small, wan smile. "The other girls told me 'whatever you do, don't go into the dressing room alone.' But there was no one here, and I didn't have much time, because my dad's waiting for me in the car and he needs to get to his second job soon."

I took out a Kleenex and handed it to her. She wiped her eyes. "Come on," I said. "Let's try on some dresses. When is your dance?"

"Tomorrow. My mom is coming with me in the afternoon, to get my hair and face done. Jim, my boyfriend is buying me flowers."

"You are going to be beautiful," I said, helping her step into the dress and fastening it up behind her. She was still mostly a child, her thin body shaking with cold, her breasts barely filling the cups of the dress. I thought how she would look tomorrow night, the colored lights dancing in her glossy hair and on the flowers her boyfriend had given her. She might marry young, have a couple of kids, work two low paying jobs to support her family and never again have her hair done or wear a dress like this. But tomorrow night she would be a princess.

Chapter Twenty-Five

I was half way home when I realized that though, for several hours, I'd been getting teenagers into dresses they would wear to a dance tomorrow night, I'd forgotten about my own event. I turned the car around and by the time I reached the 'Be a Model' store, someone was pulling the flexible door closed. I could see Mary inside sitting with her feet on a chair, sipping coffee.

"Drew," she said as I ducked in. "Did you leave something?"

"I need a dress," I said. "Can I buy two?"

"Sure," she said. "But we've dismantled the dressing room so you can't try them on. We have to fit everything into one room overnight, so we can lock it up. Hurry. We're going to be out of here in one minute."

I dashed over to the rack and in quick succession chose two dresses, one full length and one calf-length. I held them up against my body, hoping that they would fit. I couldn't try them on, and I wasn't going to risk exposing my naked body to George Lincoln's surprise attack. I went back to Mary, put twenty dollars into her hand and headed for the door.

"Drew," she said. "I meant what I said about tomorrow. If you can come in, we could sure use you."

"Thank you," I said, feeling guilty. There might be no one here to protect the girls from George Lincoln, but I'd already made my promises to Matt.

When I got home, I tried on both dresses and miraculously both fit. They were good quality, well-made garments and I wondered about someone sewing in a third world country for less than minimum wage and the huge markup a big name store would take when they sold it. I guess it didn't matter. In spite of this, the dresses on the racks would make some kids very happy. Wasn't that what really mattered in the end?

Tomorrow was Saturday, and Matt would be here bright and early to pick up both Lilli and me. I really needed to get some sleep. But the cell phone beckoned. I poured myself a soda and then sat on the couch thinking.

Ralph Kyzinski, Sara's father had said that Sara used Snapchat, so it was likely that there might not be any useful e-mails on the phone. But somewhere on this phone there could be a connection to her murderer.

The phone was charged so I opened it up. Sara had multiple apps. She was trying to lose weight, she played word games, she was on Facebook and Twitter but I had no idea what her password was. I punched up the media page where she kept her photos and saved them to my computer. There were lots of pictures of Sara and Darryl, and then shots of the mountains, lakes, trees and wild animals, a deer, raccoon, skunk, butterfly and even a few of wildflowers. There were three nude pictures of Sara, similar to the ones I'd seen in the cabin. Had Darryl seen these? He might have found them accidentally, or she could have teased him with them. If Darryl had indeed killed Sara, I might be holding his motive for the deed in my hand. He certainly had a right to be angry; he had provided the money for her to buy a car and the house for her to live in. But was he the kind of young man who would do something like that? I just didn't know.

Chapter Twenty-Six

It was now almost one-thirty at night and I hadn't packed my stuff for tomorrow. I got out my backpack and put into it three big bottles of water for Lilli and me, a T-shirt, long sleeved shirt, jeans and hiking boots. I tucked a bandana into the pack too, remembering how dusty it had been in the paper mill. What else? A fold-up bowl for Lilli and food, granola bars and nuts for me. When everything was laid out, I put on my pajamas and went to bed.

You'd think once my body hit the bed, I would have fallen right to sleep, but I didn't. For a long time, I lay awake, Lilli snoring beside me, thinking about the girls I had met today, and the girl whose body I had found in the woods. In spite of the antagonism between my parents, I'd never had to worry about having nice clothes, and for our first dance, my father had hired a limousine and paid for our dates to take us to supper. The kids I had seen yesterday might have a party thrown by their parents and held in a public place. There might be music and more dancing, but no liquor. When I was seventeen, I could get drunk regularly on my parents' booze and they never seemed the wiser. I thought of the father waiting patiently in the car in the parking lot for his daughter. Had he known what was going on in the dressing room, he might have gladly punched George Lincoln in the face. Would my father have cared that much? I think he did, but he showed it in a more restrained way.

Eventually I drifted into sleep, with thankfully no dreams.

When Matt knocked on my door the next morning, I was ready. Lilli, knowing that she was going was standing eagerly beside me. Matt was dressed in a flannel shirt and jeans with dark brown, well-used work boots. I followed him down the stairs. Hershey was in his crate in the back and the two dogs sniffed each other. I lifted Lilli up beside Hershey and we closed the door.

"We're meeting Jim and Kelly in Tupper Lake," Matt said. "And Kelly's dog Hooter."

"Hooter, like the girls who work in the restaurant wearing short shorts and low-cut T's?"

"Hooter, like Kelly thinks her dog is a hoot, and when he finds something he makes a hooting call."

"Sounds interesting."

"You'll like her."

"Will WhizBang be there?"

"Yup. Jim thinks that as long as Whiz is up to it, he will give him a chance at the game. It would be cruel to leave him at home when he has so little time left."

"What do they do for dogs with cancer?"

"Chemo. Same as for people. Whiz has just started his treatment, so he may be a little slower today."

We got to Tupper Lake and had pulled into a disused parking lot beside a long narrow building with boarded up windows that was the former bowl factory. Standing beside Jim's SUV were Jim, with WhizBang and a woman I recognized as Kelly. She was small and delicate and wore shorts, a T-shirt and army boots.

Beside her, a large, dignified standard poodle stood on a leash. I walked over and held out my hand.

"I'm Drew Morgan," I said. I pointed to Lilli just exiting the back of Matt's car. "My dog Lilliput."

"Kelly Lograin," she said. She pointed at the poodle. "Hooter."

Hershey had come out of his crate and the dogs were circling around getting to know each other. Jim had taken out a diagram showing the layout of the factory and we started setting out the practice for the day. There were areas around the factory that could be used for hide and seek, but it was clouding up and starting to rain gently. I wondered about Kelly's preference for shorts, but she seemed unaffected by the weather. The dogs were wearing the vests that identified them as search and rescue, the same ones they'd worn when we'd found Sara in the refrigerator, and possibly the same ones they'd worn when they found me. The last time we'd trained, it had just been too hot for the vests, but it was now mid-September, and I knew that wearing the vest signals to the dog that he's working, even if the 'work' is practice in an unused factory.

We practiced all morning in the building with all the dogs getting to search out all the owners. It was dirty work and would have been impossible for someone with claustrophobia. Hershey, WhizBang and Hooter were all rewarded with Kongs. Lilliput had only a ball, but I had brought plenty of treats. By noon, we were leaning against the side of Matt's SUV, all of us dirty and tired. Kelly had positioned herself next to Matt, sometimes putting her hand on his arm to make a point when they were talking. It was the kind of familiarity that old friends have, not I hoped, the familiarity of lovers.

"What do you do for a living?" Kelly asked, looking at me.

"Various things," I said. "Right now I'm teaching art to high school kids three days a week."

"Not much money in that."

"The other days I work in a motel in Saranac."

I expected a look, but she said nothing. "What do you do, Kelly?"

"I'm with the Army in Watertown. Fort Drum."

"She's a Sergeant," Jim said. "She's off duty so you don't need to salute."

I looked over at the tiny woman who looked fragile enough to be pulled over sideways by her sixty- pound dog. She was tough enough to wear shorts in the fall. Tough enough for lots of things.

"Don't let my job intimidate you," Kelly said. "We do what we can to make a living."

"I worked for an ad agency in New York City before moving up here and I still sell my art at Adirondack Made." This was all I could muster in the I've-got- a- more- prestigious- job- than you- have department.

Kelly only nodded. Jim had moved away and was throwing balls for WhizBang, who now that I watched him, seemed to move more slowly.

"You guys hungry?" Jim said. "I am."

"We'll meet you at Billy's Deli," Matt said.

We had lunch and then Matt took Lilli and me home. When we were sitting in the parking lot to my apartment, he reached over and gently kissed me. "I'm looking forward to tonight," he said.

I smiled. It was fun to be looking forward to a dance with a good-looking guy.

That evening I took extra care with my toilette. I don't normally wear a lot of makeup, but with my newly coiffed hair, it seemed like a nice idea. I had decided on a teal blue, full-length strapless gown with silver spangles along the top and in a panel down the side. With the dress I was wearing flesh colored heels, that I'd purchased, at three times the price of the gown, and carried a tiny silver purse, just big enough to hold a credit card. A silver cashmere shawl would protect me from drafts.

"Wow." Matt said, when he saw me. "You look fantastic."

I gave a small bow. "Not bad yourself." He was wearing a white tux with a teal green cummerbund, tie and a matching handkerchief. His hair was slicked back. In his hand he carried a plastic box with a Gardenia. "Let me fit it in your hair," he said, pulling the flower out and reaching toward me. He was so close I could smell his aftershave. Our cheeks were inches apart and if he just turned his head, our lips would meet. He turned his head. I closed my eyes and felt his lips on mine, warm, persuasive. We'd never slept together, but at that moment if he'd asked I would have said yes. He pulled away.

"We'll never get to the dance this way," he said. He looked at me. "But I wouldn't mind continuing this later."

I nodded. We headed out the door, and he held the door while I got myself into his SUV.

The dance was being held at the Lake Placid Hilton which seemed to have every light in the place blazing. When we stepped inside there were balloons and streamers hanging from the ceiling, tables decorated with sparkles and candles tucked into the corner. Two huge posters, each one featuring a grinning dog wearing his search and rescue vest decorated the stage on which a podium stood. Behind the podium a band was warming up. We went over to the bar and got our drinks and then stood around for a moment. I didn't know any of these people, but Matt did, so I was introduced politely and made small talk, and then it was time to go to our tables and be served supper.

As we were finishing our dessert a man came to the podium and the mike was turned up. A movie screen behind him descended from the ceiling but remained blank.

"Ladies and gentlemen," the speaker said. "I want to thank you all for coming tonight and for the contributions you have already made and will continue to make to a good cause. Search and rescue people, the teams of man and animal, do the job because they feel it is important, not for the money, because, in truth, no amount of money can compensate for the effort it takes to rescue someone. A search and rescue canine and his person endure heat, cold, dust, wind, insects, treacherous footing and potential death. Many S & R people help pay for their own transportation to areas where they are needed. They pay for their own food and housing and that of their dogs. Your contribution tonight won't wholly compensate those people, but it will help them deliver needed services to areas where they are important. I ask that you be generous."

The lights went down and a picture went up on the screen. It was of a German shepherd balanced delicately on a beam above a pick-up-sticks pile of boards. He was backlit, and looking down into the rubble below. The picture changed. A little boy, dirty, with tears in his eyes, his arm around the black lab who had found him. The next slide was of an old woman, sitting against a tree with a Mylar blanket over her shoulders, the dog who had found her, a Basset hound, sitting beside her. There were many more rescue pictures. The last was of a woman her hair askew, her face streaked with dirt sitting against a tree while two dogs sat beside her. It took me a moment to realize it was me.

I felt the tears start. "Oh God," I said. I could see Matt and Jim in the picture, and Hershey and WhizBang.

"I think I'm going to cry," I said. The M.C. was saying something but I wasn't paying attention. "They want you to stand, Drew," Matt said. "You're one of our success stories."

I stood and people clapped.

"I feel like a fraud," I said. "It's not me they should be clapping for, it's you guys."

"We get our reward in other ways," Matt whispered.

The M.C. was talking again. "We can't show you photos of all the search and rescue people worldwide because there are so many, so here are just a few." On the screen flashed a photo of a tiny white-haired woman and a giant black poodle. "Grace and Harley," the speaker said. A black man with a border collie looking up at him adoringly. "Jeff and Cody." A tired-looking man with a dirty face, wearing a harness and a hard hat sitting on the ground, his feet stretched out before him and beside him a yellow lab. "Rafael and Amigo." A dozen pictures flashed on the screen. All of these people with their dogs, lifelong partnerships every one of them.

"These men and women you see, and many that we have not shown you, are the ones who go out into the dirt and heat and the danger to help us find our loved ones. These are the people you are supporting tonight," the speaker said. "Please be generous."

They passed a hard-hat around and we all put in money. Then the band struck up "Let me Call You Sweetheart," and people got up to dance. Matt held out his hand and when I rose, he led me to the floor, pulling me into his arms. You can tell a lot about a man by dancing with him. I put my head on his chest and he pulled me close. I could hear his heartbeat, feel his muscles working. It was heavenly.

"People are watching us," he said.

I pulled my head up to look around. "They are not."

"Well maybe not now, but when you were introduced and got up, half the guys were wondering who that gorgeous female was, and what had I done to get her."

I pulled away to look at his face. "OK, I'll bite. What *did* you do to get me?"

"I have no idea. Except that when we found you in the woods, it was my lucky day."

I could have told him that luck had nothing to do with whether a relationship would work or not. For two people to stay together, and support and commit to each other---that took work.

The music had stopped and the band leader stepped up to the mike. "We're taking a little break folks. Have another drink, schmooze with your neighbors, take your dog for a walk. We'll be back soon."

"What would you like to drink?" Matt asked.

179

"Moscato," I said. Across the room I could see Jud Weinstein turn and start walking toward me.

"I'm going to the ladies' room," I said. "I'll meet you back at the table." I streaked toward the bathrooms, catching up with Jud on the way. When we were outside the doors to the bathrooms, I asked, "What are you doing here?"

"I have as much right to be here as you do. Actually I'm on assignment. Lots of big money here tonight." He leaned in. "I'm waiting for Sara's cell phone, Drew. You promised."

"I haven't had a minute," I lied. "I've been with Matt all day."

"Are you fraternizing with cops, Drew?"

"He's a park ranger."

"Same thing. Listen, I really want to take a look at that phone. If you're done with it, I'll come over and get it, and I don't care who sees me at your house. You understand don't you?"

He had raised his voice and several women coming out of the bathroom glanced over at us. In the distance, I could see Matt coming toward us.

"Get the hell out of here now Jud and let me enjoy the dance." I said. I didn't even wait to see whether he'd gone, just ducked into the ladies' room.

Once inside, I stood before the mirror trying to work out a plan. I had got rid of Jud temporarily, but that didn't mean he wouldn't be around tomorrow or the next day. What the hell had I gotten myself into?

When I came out of the bathroom, Matt was waiting.

"What did that guy want?" he asked.

"Nothing, really. He's a reporter who was asking questions about search and rescue dogs."

"It didn't look like a friendly conversation."

I decided to tell Matt at least part of the truth. "Jud Weinstein caught up with me after I got out of the hospital and wanted to know about my experience being lost in the woods. Then he saw us again after we found Sara's body. I think he's writing a story about the whole thing."

"The whole thing? Your experience being lost in the woods, or the murder?"

"Both," I said.

"I heard that his girlfriend worked for the police department, but they fired her when they found she was sharing confidential information," Matt said. "If you want my advice, stay away from him."

I wish I'd heard the advice weeks ago.

We danced a few more times, but a lot of the magic had gone out of the evening. When the dance finally ended, Matt led me to the car, held the door while I got in, but then instead of starting the car he leaned over and said. "Would you come to my place for a drink?"

I hesitated. A drink could lead to any number of things, and I had a dog at home who would be waiting patiently. I looked over at this man who up to this point had been kind and considerate and only a gentleman. What the heck. If it was only going to be a drink I would say yes. If it were going to be more than that, I might say yes, too.

We drove to a small two story house overlooking the lake, probably one of those homes with 'cure porches' for the tuberculosis patients. Matt unlocked the door and we were in a 1930's era house, with a small living room with table and chairs, a kitchen to one side, a den on the other and a stairway leading to the second floor. The place was decorated with heavy mission-style furniture, the darkness relieved by several oil paintings of forests and one of the Grand Canyon. On a chest stood a collection of photos, many of them of people with their dogs. His search and rescue friends.

"This is nice," I said.

"It's a Sears house. In the 1920's and 1930's people could get a kit to build a house." He led me to a nook in the wall holding a carved bear. "This was a telephone nook," he said. "When people bought these houses, they sometimes bought furniture to go with them as well." He waved his hand toward a couch with wooden arms and old-fashioned plaid-covered seats. "The good thing is this stuff is practically indestructible."

The place needed brightening. Instead of all this dark furniture, it could use more colorful rugs or artwork. A woman's touch. Was I volunteering to be that woman?

"Wine," Matt said. "I did promise you that, didn't I." He moved to a miniscule kitchen that held a stove, a refrigerator, a sink and a microwave. The cupboards didn't look like they held much.

"How do you get along in such a small space?"

He was reaching into the refrigerator for the bottles. "To tell you the truth, except for firing up the barbecue to cook a steak or nuking something frozen, I'm not much of a cook."

He had turned with the bottles. I was standing right there. Hershey had tucked himself right behind me and there was no way I could move. I realized that I didn't want to move. Matt reached behind him and put down the bottles. Then he turned back toward me.

"I have told you how beautiful you are, haven't I?"

"I don't mind your saying it again," I said. My heart was beating fiercely. He had pulled me toward him and was kissing me possessively, in a way I hadn't expected. But I was feeling the same. I was impatient and needy and it didn't matter that we'd only known each other a short time, because at that moment I wanted to know Matt Waring intimately.

He was kissing his way down, over my throat, my shoulders, over the tops of my breasts.

"Wait," I said, and reached behind to unhook the dress and then the bra.

My fingers were in his hair as he moved down to my breasts. I needed more of him. I needed all of him.

"We could go upstairs," he whispered. "If you are willing."

"I am very willing," I said. But moving upstairs meant pulling away. Eventually we found ourselves on the second floor in a tiny bedroom. He was wearing entirely too much. And I was wearing entirely too much. I could hear Hershey bounding up the stairs toward the bedroom, and just before he could come in, Matt kicked the door shut on the dog so we could get down to the business of making love.

Chapter Twenty-Seven

I woke to light coming in through the window and it took me a minute to remember where I was. In a corner was a chair with my dress carelessly thrown over it and on the floor were my panties and bra. I remembered the feel of Matt's hands on my body, the feeling of utter joy as we made love. Matt was a wonderful lover and a caring man. Had I really committed myself to him after one night? I could smell coffee brewing, so Matt must be downstairs. I'd just been looking around for something to cover myself with when the door opened.

Matt came in, carrying a tray on which were two cups, a coffee pot and a plate of scones. Hershey was right behind him, coming up to the bed to put his head on the mattress.

"Get away," Matt said, pushing the dog from the bed. He put down the tray then he sat beside me.

"Good morning, beautiful," he said, kissing me.

"This is a treat," I said, looking at the scones. "You didn't make these yourself, did you?"

"I only eat what I can nuke or throw on a fire. But the bakery down the street makes wonderful scones."

"The bakery that is closed today?"

"Well yes. The bakery that *is* closed today. I got them yesterday."

185

I took a bite of the scones that were buttery and sweet and loaded with blueberries. It was flattering that he'd planned ahead, just in case I decided to stay the night. What would he have done if I'd said no? For one thing, he'd have had to eat all these scones by himself.

"It's Sunday," he said, between sips of coffee. "What's on your agenda for today?"

"I need to get home and feed my dog." I glanced over at the dress. "And if we're going to do anything besides dance, I need to change."

He leaned over and kissed me on the cheek. Then he worked his way down the side of my face to my neck and the top of my breast just peeking out from above the sheet I was holding. "We could have a different agenda," he said.

I pulled away. "If we start this again, I'll never get home and Lilli is waiting for me."

He leaned back against the headboard. "We could go canoeing and take the dogs. I've got an old aluminum beater behind the house. We could take a picnic lunch and go up to Little Saranac."

"Sounds like fun," I said.

By the time we got back to my house it was almost ten. At the front door, I tried to be as quiet as possible, knowing that Mrs. Steen was on the first floor and would be aware that I'd been out all night. On the other hand, she was only my landlady and I was a grown woman, allowed to do whatever I damned well felt like. When we got upstairs to the apartment, Lilli was frantically happy to see us. She had knocked over her water bowl, there was no food, and she was desperate to pee.

"I'll take her out," Matt said.

I rushed into the bedroom to change. Quickly I got myself out of the dress, the strapless bra and panties and into a pair of jeans and a long- sleeved top. It was September, so even on a sunny day like this, it might be cool on the water. I found some sneakers and then I searched all over the place for a hat. I could hear Lilli in the other room, so Matt must be back from the walk. Finally, I found a sweater and a hat. I opened the door. The dogs were sprawled on the floor. Matt was sitting on the couch.

He turned toward me, his look stony. In his hand was Sara's pink cell phone, the one that I'd left sitting beside the computer.

"Where did you get this?" he asked.

I went to the kitchen and poured myself a cup of coffee, then returned to sit in a chair opposite.

"You haven't answered my question. Or maybe by saying nothing, you have answered it."

"You wouldn't even know that Sara was dead if it weren't for me. She would still be lying in the woods, rotting away in that old refrigerator, and the person who killed her would be probably chuckling to himself that he'd gotten away with murder."

"I doubt that murderer's chuckle."

"Ok, maybe not chuckling. But feeling smug, feeling powerful. He killed a young girl, one with her whole future ahead of her. Are we going to let him get away with it?" My tears were falling now uncontrollable and uncontrolled. "I couldn't save Carley and I couldn't save Sara, but I can help find who killed her."

"Drew," he said, rising so he was standing facing me. "Finding a murderer isn't that easy. Sometimes murder just happens. People are in the wrong place, and the murderer just happens to be there. Or people are in a relationship with someone who has uncontrolled anger. I'm not sure there is anything a person can do to prevent being killed when the killer is intent on doing it."

"Sara contacted me, Matt. I can't just walk away," I said widening the space between us. Just hours ago, we had been lovers and now we were facing off against each other. But I needed to stand my ground.

"Drew," he said. "You are not a policeman. You are not a detective. You have no idea how dangerous this work can be. Not only is your meddling interfering with the work of people who know what they're doing, but you are putting yourself in harm's way. How do you know the murderer isn't still out there, trying to protect himself from being found and eager to stop anyone from finding him?"

We were quiet for a moment. Matt was turning the phone over and over in his hands.

"You didn't say where you got this," he said. "You can't deny it's hers. I looked at the pictures."

"One of my students Darryl Boxer told me where she lived."

"Do the police know this?"

I shook my head.

"How did Darryl Boxer know her whereabouts?

"He helped her come up here from Pennsylvania and found her a place to live. It was the cabin where Dr. LeBrun was living."

"And where he was shot. My God. And she was there all the time?"

"I guess she was."

Matt put the phone down on the coffee table, without glancing my way. Finally he looked up but the affection in his eyes was gone. "You need to go to the police, Drew. This phone is an important part of the investigation."

I nodded. Matt reached into his pocket, drew out a card and wrote a phone number on the back. "Call Jim Weims tomorrow. First thing." Then he rose from the couch; Hershey rose too.

"I'll let myself out," he said.

Chapter Twenty- Eight

The next day was Monday, my art day at the school, so I had time in the morning to talk with Jim. I called the station and was put right through. Matt must have already had 'the conversation' with him.

"You can come right now, Drew," he said. "Matt said you have Sara's cell phone, and more information."

After I hung up the phone, I called Jud and told him the situation about the phone and the pictures. "I'm taking it down to the station now," I said.

"Drew," he pleaded. "I want those pictures. Just e-mail them to me."

"If you publish them, the police will know where they came from," I said.

"I'll tell them I found the phone first, then I shared it with you."

"And you'll say you discovered the cabin?"

"Sure,"

I was getting into deep doo-doo here. Even if Jud did lie for me, it was no guarantee that one or both of us wouldn't end up in jail for interfering with an investigation. But I wanted to be rid, not only of the phone, but of Jud and of everything about this murder case. On the other hand, the victim had reached out to me.

"I'm going now, Jud. Can you meet me at the police station?"

"Now? Drew I'm working."

"If I have to do this alone, I will deliver the phone to the police and you won't see the pictures on it. If you come with me, I will e-mail you what I found on the phone."

"Before or after?"

"After."

"God damn it, woman," he said. "OK."

I waited outside the police station until I saw Jud's rattletrap vehicle, which in spite of its aged appearance was better than my piece of junk. He got out of the car and we walked into the station together. Jim was waiting for us.

The three of us went back to his office and sat. I took the cell phone out of my pocket and put it on the desk. Jud glanced at me, warily, as though he still wasn't sure that he could trust me.

"We'll have to fingerprint you," Jim said looking at Jud. "We already have yours, Drew."

I nodded.

"So you've looked at this?"

I nodded. "She used Snapchat for her e-mail, so there isn't much there, but there are pictures." He was fiddling with the phone. I could see his eyes widen as he came to the nude pictures. Jud leaned forward to look.

"You've seen these?" Jim asked.

I nodded.

"So, tell me how you found this?" he asked.

I looked at Jud, wondering how good he was at lying on the spot. Then I spoke up, telling him about my conversation with Darryl Boxer, about calling Jud and finding Dr. LeBrun's cabin."

Jim nodded "Dr. LeBrun's death was my investigation. I know exactly where the place is." He picked up the phone, ready to make a call, and then decided against it, possibly because we were right there. "Did you touch anything?"

I nodded and he sighed heavily. We described what we had found and why we thought Sara was living in the camp.

"Is there anything else?"

"I know that she was driving an old red Volvo, but it wasn't at the cabin."

"How do you know she drove a red Volvo?"

I couldn't remember. I had talked to several people and any one of them could have told me, but then I would have been revealing to Jim Weims that we were involved with witnesses in a criminal investigation. "I think Darryl told me," I said. "You should look behind his bright green trailer at Garden Acres. But be careful of the Rottweiler."

Jim had taken out a pad of paper and was writing something on it. He looked at Jud. "I should warn you that you cannot publish anything about this case until it is over. It's an ongoing investigation. We can't have reporters revealing confidential information."

"Damn," Jud said. "I was hoping to write a book about the murder."

"I'll tell you what I will do. If you will hold off publishing anything more until this is solved, I will help you sort out what happened. Until then, you need to stay away from the camp where Sara was living, away from where her body was found, away from anything pertaining to the crime scene and any witnesses to the crime. Do I have your promise?"

Reluctantly Jud nodded.

"You need to do the same, Drew," he said. "Leave the detecting to the professionals."

"OK."

We were dismissed. Jud and I walked back to his car in silence. "I'm sorry," I said finally.

"Yeah."

"He's right. We aren't detectives."

"But we found where Sara was living. How come they didn't know about that?"

I shrugged. "Darryl Boxer hated the police, because his father had a meth lab and has been arrested."

"I am writing this book, no matter what happens."

I nodded. "I will e-mail you the pictures," I said.

That afternoon in my art class Darryl Boxer was absent again, and when asked where he was I simply got shrugs. I had e-mailed pictures of Darryl's artwork to my dad and gotten an enthusiastic response, although my dad had not said that he would help Darryl mount a show or would recommend him to a teacher. In the end, I wondered what in fact I'd done to help the boy. The class was eager to see me, and their eagerness lifted my spirits. At least in this one small way I could change the lives of some young people.

Chapter Twenty-Nine

On Thursday I went early to my job at the Sleepy Inn motel. It was now late September and the leaves had already started turning colors. I had been spending my free hours painting and I think I had some beautiful pieces that I could try to sell. But Adirondack Made was already reducing their hours and in another month they would be closed. If I were going to be an artist earning money from my skill, I needed to go farther afield.

I was halfway through cleaning the first room when there was a call on my cell phone. It was Arlette asking me to come to her office. *Oh oh*, I thought. *Not good.*

"Sit down, Drew," Arlette said when I was in her office. I sat. "You've been a good employee. And if there were any way I could keep you working here I would."

Damn, she was firing me. "As you know, things slow down in the winter, and I just don't have the business to keep two girls on." She looked down at her desk. "You can finish out the week, and then I am sorry, but I don't need you anymore."

Shit. Shit. Shit. I needed this job. The only salary I had now was what I earned from teaching three days a week at the high school, and that wasn't going to be enough. But I wasn't going to beg; it would do me no good. I rose and slowly went back to the room.

I sat on the bed I was supposed to be making and looked at the walls of the room. What was I doing with my life anyway? I'd come to the Adirondacks to paint and had done very little of that.

Instead I'd tried to eke out a living selling stuff, cleaning toilets, and teaching but none of those things was a full time job. Maybe it was time to go back to New York.

That evening I called my dad. Crow is a tough meal to chew, but I had to do it. I told him I had done some good work recently and would he consider putting one or two of my pictures in his gallery. He was reluctant at first, saying that he preferred avant-garde stuff, but I told him I would e-mail him pictures. I wasn't going to beg here either. When I hung up the phone I sorted through the pictures I'd done and picked out six of the best. Then I photographed them and e-mailed them off. There might be other galleries that were looking for artists, so I sat down at my computer and, for a half hour waded through galleries in the northeast part of the country where I could reasonably ship my stuff. I e-mailed pictures to four of them. I turned off the computer, pushed a dish into the microwave, poured a glass of wine and sat down to watch TV.

I was half way through a show that I was only moderately interested in when an ad for Lincoln Retail Properties came on the screen, and there big as life was George Lincoln, standing in front of a brand-new Adirondack-style camp. Several more pictures flashed on the screen, mostly new houses, but some were businesses, Pizza parlors, tourist shops and motels, including The Sleepy Inn. The motel I'd just been fired from.

Turning off the TV, I went to my computer and Googled George Lincoln. The photographs of houses and businesses on the front of the website were the same as those I'd seen on TV. A sidebar announced "About George" and when I clicked on that, there was a series of pictures: George on the golf course, George with girls at "Be a Model for a Day," George presenting a check to the Chamber of Commerce, George standing beside the Sheriff in front of a new police vehicle, and posing beside two little kids in baseball uniforms with Lincoln Properties emblazoned on the front. There were lots of other pictures. George and his wife lived in an apartment in New York City but spent every summer in the Adirondacks, and they seemed to be generous donors wherever they lived. The last picture was of George and his blonde, model wife who looked to be about ten years younger than he was. Did she know what kind of guy she had married? What would she say if someone told her that her husband pushed himself on fourteen and fifteen year old girls who were helpless to defend themselves?

It wasn't doing me any good to moan about the fact that a rich prick had convinced my boss to fire me, because I'd told him he couldn't harass teenagers. I needed an income. I could talk to Jay Johnson, the high school principal and see if they could up my teaching hours, but it was a long shot. I could go back to New York City, sleep in my father's apartment under the steely eye of his girlfriend and risk seeing Scott, his wife and new baby. Or I could stay here and tough it out.

On Friday, the last day of my job at the motel, I left work at the regular time, aware that I now had only the three days of work at the high school to support me. To get my mind of my troubles, I took Lilli for a long walk along the lake, and then as a treat, I bought myself a latte and sat on a bench just looking at the view. Fall in the Adirondacks is one of the most paintable seasons. The mountains in the distance were a soft ultramarine blue under a cobalt sky, with trees of cadmium red, warm orange, alizarin crimson, quinacridone gold and burnt umber. I wished I'd brought my paints, but all I could do was look and try to remember.

Two little girls strolled past me and settled onto a bench nearby. They were alike enough to be twins but not twins. Even though their eyes, hair color and height were similar I could see each of them had a strong quest to be unique. One girl had her hair braided in dreadlocks, the ends of the braids decorated with colorful beads. The other girl's slightly curly hair was done in a conventional page boy. The dreadlocked girl wore a brightly-colored blouse and dark tights; her sister wore a blue dress with a prim collar. They were, through their clothing, advertising their personalities. One girl was adventurous and bold, gobbling up life like an endless dessert and the other was cautious and conforming, waiting for her sibling to pave the way before she put a foot forward. Carley and Me. Me and Carley

I was thirteen again, standing in the alley behind the grocery store with Carley taking a puff of a joint. "Come on Drew. Just try it," she said, as she slumped down against the brick wall giggling.

"We'll be arrested if they catch us."

"Come on, Drew. Live a little."

And Carley, in her low cut blouse, dancing at a party, the boys she would toss aside like used paper, ogling her from the sidelines, while I sat envious and admiring all at once.

And as I imagined her on the last day of her life. Carley walking home from the grocery store, swinging her hips, maybe singing to herself. She would be wearing something provocative, tight jeans and a low-cut blouse. Even as she egged men on, she was an innocent. In this scenario a man, recently released from prison pulls up beside her in a car, and calls out the open window. "Can you give me directions?"

Carley shakes her head. She tells him she's not from around here and doesn't know the area. But the man stops the car, hops out, dances after my sister. He isn't bad looking, and he has a line of conversation that he's used before. The girl is hot, but it's not sexual excitement he feels but something that will be released when he hears her scream for mercy. But right now all that is in the future. He can't just snatch her on a public street. She has to be willing to go with him. So he is friendly, open, and needy. He needs to get to his sisters. He thinks he knows the way, but he isn't sure. If she could get in the car with him, she can help him find the house and then they can go out for coffee later. Carley gets into the car.

I don't think about what happens next, even though during the trial, the killer spent a long time bragging about the details. All I know is that Carley, the younger sister who was never afraid, and who had held my hand and urged me to take a chance, is gone. When she died, I fell into a dark void that took me a long time to claw my way back from. What saved me was months of creating paintings that were black and grey with only a spot of red. I won't say that my art saved me. You can never really erase a scar like that, but slowly I came out of my grief and was able to go on.

I came out of my daydream and looked at my watch. It was still early evening, and I needed to go home and get my paints and work on something I might be able to sell, but still I sat. The two little girls had moved on, but my thoughts were still on my sister.

Saturday morning, September 23. I was still slopping around in my ratty pajamas, trying to figure out what to do with my life now that I had only one job to support me, when a knock came on the door. I got up from the couch, pushing Lilli's head off my lap and opened it. Matt Waring was standing there, and beside him was Hershey.

"I tried to call," he said. "But you aren't answering your phone."

My cell was still in my purse and no doubt the battery was dead. I pushed some magazines and clothing off a chair and he sat down, Hershey at his feet. Lilli went over to Hershey and the two sniffed each other.

"I want to apologize," he said slowly. "I'm not sorry about what I said the other day, just the way I said it." He leaned closer. "I know you think that solving this murder can somehow bring your sister back. It can't. I wish I could change what happened."

He got up and came to sit beside me on the couch. "I've never met anyone who has survived what you did. I've never met anyone who'd fought for her life the way you did, who didn't give up. I think it was what drew me to you, it was what made me... care about you."

I nodded. It was nice that he cared. I was half in love with him too, but I wasn't sure whether what I'd done had doused a fire that had been burning nicely, cooling it forever.

"I don't want anything to happen to you," he said.

"I lost my job at the motel," I said.

Matt nodded. "So your plan for today is to hang around in your PJ's drinking coffee and feeling sorry for yourself?"

"No."

"No?"

"No. My plan for today is to hang around in my PJ's drinking wine and as soon as I'm drunk enough not to care, I'm going back to bed."

"Come on Drew. You've never been a quitter. You're a smart woman; you'll find something."

"I'm glad you think I'm a smart woman."

"Get dressed. You'll feel better when you're out of here."

He was right. My apartment was small, crowded, and desperately in need of a good cleaning, not a place that would cheer anyone up.

"Give me a minute to get dressed," I said.

When we got into the SUV, Matt said. "How about Juniper Pond? It's a beautiful place, near where we found you."

"What about the blowdown? Has that been cleared away?"

"Not all of it, but I know my way in the woods and there are trails we can use."

I took a deep breath, and tried not to let the memory of being lost overwhelm me.

"We'll be together?" I asked.

"Like Hansel and Gretel. We don't even need bread crumbs; we've got the dogs." He looked at me. "You've got to get back on the horse, Drew. If you don't face your fear of getting lost, you'll never regain the thing that gives you joy."

We drove to a parking lot, one that was vaguely familiar. A front-end loader was parked at the far end.

"Have we been here before?"

"The day we found Sara, we parked here," he said. "We're taking a different route today. I want to show you Juniper Pond."

I took a deep breath, and grabbed my backpack. Matt let the dogs out of the back and we headed into the woods. I tried to breathe, to push away the dread that seemed to be my reaction to the trees around me. I vaguely remembered taking this same trail about a month ago. Nothing was going to happen. I was with a man who knew the woods the way I knew my apartment and with two dogs that wouldn't let me get lost. Hershey and Lilliput were off leash and the dogs bounded ahead of us, every once in a while dashing into the woods after some creature and dashing back. The sharp scent of leaves underfoot rose to meet me; overhead a woodpecker drummed and the light through the trees cast a pale yellow glow. I grabbed my phone and snapped a picture of the trees, then another of a red newt on the trail that skittered away as soon as I got close.

"So you lost your job," Matt said.

"I was thinking about going back to New York City, bunking in with my dad and trying to get another job in advertising," I said.

Matt looked at me. "I hope you don't. I know living here is rough, especially in the winter, but personally, I like knowing you."

"I like knowing you, too."

We walked on companionably in silence. "Where are the dogs?" I asked.

"Hershey," Matt called. "Here boy."

"Lilliput." I whistled. Neither dog appeared.

Matt whistled loudly and suddenly Hershey appeared running down the trail toward us, Lilli right behind him.

"What's got into you guys," Matt said, reaching down to pat his dog. Hershey sat.

When we started walking again, Hershey had moved out in front of Matt, Lilli beside him. Hershey kept looking back to make sure we were following. Clearly the dogs were trying to tell us something. They led us down the trail for about a hundred yards, then stopped and sat, waiting for us to catch up.

When we were behind the dogs, they turned and led us into the woods. It wasn't a regular trail; there were roots, hidden by the leaves, and depressions that could have tripped me up. We walked on for a while through thick brush, following the dogs. Suddenly Hershey stopped and lay down, and Lilli, following his lead, did the same.

We got to the place where the dogs were lying close to a depression in the soft ground made by a fallen tree. Matt went first, peering into the hole.

"Jesus," he breathed. He took out a penlight and played it over the area. I leaned in. There staring at us with sightless eyes was Celestina.

"She's the medium who told me to look for Sara," I said.

Matt leaned in to see her closer, but pulled back. "Whew. She's been here for a while."

Hershey was dancing around, clearly proud of his find. Matt reached into his pocket and pulled out a treat. I gave Lilli something too.

"We need to call the police," Matt said. He took out his phone and I watched as he started dialing a number. He asked for Jim Weims, giving him specific directions to where we were. When he'd hung up, he said. "We'll have to be here for a while. I hope you don't mind."

We settled ourselves on the ground. Matt opened his pack and pulled out two water bottles, a small bowl and a couple of granola bars. He handed me a bar, poured water into the bowl and watched as the dogs took turns drinking. He closed the pack and put it on the ground between us. Behind me, I could still smell Celestina's decomposing body. We needed to be close to the body so we could point it out to Jim, but this closeness was becoming uncomfortable.

The wind had come up, rustling the dry leaves above me, and scattering them on the ground. I felt a momentary pang of fear. I looked at Matt.

"It's not going to happen again, Drew. Things like the microburst are a once in a lifetime event."

I looked over at Lilli and Hershey. Hershey was snoring. If anything happened here, I could trust both these dogs.

"When did you first meet Celestina?" Matt asked.

"My landlady, Mrs. Steen, wanted me to go with her to see this medium," I began and told him the whole story of our encounter. "Mrs. Steen thought she was a fake, but I don't know, she seemed to know things that no one else would know. We went to see her at the end of July, and even though she asked me to come back to see her again, I never went. Then in mid-August, after we found Sara, Celestina's daughter called me to say she was missing. Do you know if the police ever tried to find her?"

"Jim thought she was a fake, too," Matt said. "I don't know what the police did. They may have thought she had just moved away."

"Her car was there when her daughter went to the house. Why would someone want to kill her?"

"Jim said she was selling phony insurance to old people. Maybe one of her former customers caught up with her?"

"A senior citizen murdering her? Come on, Matt. How would they know where she was?"

"Didn't Jud Weinstein do an article about her?"

"Yeah. But the Journal has a very local readership."

We sat in silence, listening to bird call and the wind rustling the trees. Celestina. had given me her card, asking me to call her and I'd never done that. Then she'd called again, saying it was urgent and asking me to visit and I'd never gone. Had the thing she wanted to tell me, been the thing that had got her killed? And if I *had* gone to see her, would I be the person now lying dead in the woods? A shiver ran through me. I needed to be more careful. To get my mind off the dead body lying behind me, I looked down at Matt's backpack lying on the ground between us, and the patches he'd sewn on the back.

"What's a 46'r?" I asked. In truth, I was just making conversation.

"Someone who has hiked all 46 of the four-thousand foot peaks in the Adirondacks. I'm a winter 46'r too."

"Wow."

"I expect, with all the walking I do for my job that I've hiked some of these high peaks eight or ten times over." He opened the granola bar and began eating. I took the water bottle and drank.

"My sister and I learned to swim in Lake Flower," I said. "Once she stepped into a spring hole and almost drowned. My grandfather jumped in, fully clothed to rescue her."

I heard footsteps and looked up to see Jim and a stranger striding through the trees toward us. They were followed by a forest ranger.

"Hi Carl," Matt said to the ranger.

"Aren't you the lucky one," Carl said to Matt. "Two murders in one season."

Matt stood up and I followed. "This is Drew Morgan."

Carl looked at me. "The girl who was lost in the woods."

I pulled out several compasses that I had hanging around my neck, three of the half dozen I now owned. "I'm covered," I said.

"If you got Matt with you, you're covered," Carl said, watching as Jim and the coroner started to remove Celestina from her hole. "EMT's are here with a stretcher," Carl said.

Jim came over and sat with us for a while, asking us how we'd found the body. "I may call you later to ask you more questions," he said to me. Then he rose and went back to the body. By now there were men in uniform milling around, snapping pictures of the body, putting out little yellow flags.

"They don't need us any more," Matt said. "We should probably go."

We called the dogs and walked back down the trail toward the parking lot, which was now crowded with vehicles.

"Want to go out for lunch?" Matt said.

"Sure." I needed something to take away the sight of Celestina, lying on the ground, her body already starting to rot and being devoured by animals.

Chapter Thirty

Janet Linden, the woman who ran the catering service for Billy's Deli called me that night, reminding me that she had a large party scheduled for Friday, a week from today and needed wait staff. Was I still available?

"Sure," I said, the thought of dollars dancing through my head. I still had a little money in the bank, but that was slowly being eroded away.

"The uniform is a white shirt and dark pants," Janet said. "You've got those don't you? And no sneakers. Dark shoes. Our customer wants us to look decent." She gave me an address and told me that the party would start at four but she wanted me there at three-thirty to help set up. She named a fee that though not exorbitant, would help me get through the month.

I still hadn't decided whether to move back to the city, and I'd made a few tentative trips to Watertown looking for something in the advertising business. I hadn't found anything in my field yet, but a few places in the mall said they might be looking for extra help at Christmas. Christmas. It was only September. Could I last until Christmas without an income?

On the morning of the day I was due to work, I set it up with Mrs. Steen to care for Lilli. An article about the death of Celestina had appeared the previous day in the newspaper, and I recognized Jud's style.

"I expect it was one of her 'customers,' " Mrs. Steen said. "One of them that she cheated."

"Someone would murder her because she cheated them out of ten dollars? I don't think so," I said.

"You don't know what it's like. You go to someone expecting to hear about your loved one, and she gives you nothing. Not a thing."

"We found Sara Kyzinski because of Celestina," I said. "Without her I'd never have convinced Jim and Matt to bring the dogs into the woods."

"Well that's different. She didn't actually *find* the girl did she?"

It was no use. I couldn't win. As a result I was very humble and grateful with Mrs. Steen. I suppose I could have called Matt, but that seemed like an imposition. Mrs. Steen was just downstairs; it would not be much trouble to feed and walk Lilli.

"I will be back by eight o'clock at the latest," I said, handing her forty dollars. "This job will help me continue to stay here."

Mrs. Steen nodded. I hoped she wanted me to stay in the apartment because I was a good tenant, but I think the truth was that with winter coming on, it would be harder for her to get anyone else. Taking care of Lilli while I worked would be beneficial to us both.

I drove to the address, a large two-story Adirondack style house with floor to ceiling windows looking out over the shores of a lake. I drove past an open metal gate and parked my car, noticing as I did so, that the whole yard was surrounded by a chain link fence. What was this guy walling out? Bears? Deer? Raccoons? Moose? It seemed strange to build a house in a pristine spot like this and then demonstrate your fear of nature by putting up a fence. A van and a tiny Volkswagen were already in the parking lot, and I could see an open door near the back of the house that led into a kitchen.

"Drew," Janet said, coming out the door. "Help me carry things in, will you?"

A young man of college age followed her out of the kitchen, and together we went to Janet's van. The young man lifted a heavy box of wine from the back, and I picked up a cardboard box. Together we walked back into a kitchen large enough to cook for a small restaurant.

"Put the box there," Janet said to me. "Tim, you're going to be in here, at the bar." She led us to a living room which was three times the size of my apartment. Above us stretched the rafters of the building, held up by enormous trusses, below which were log-beams, still holding some of their original bark. It was like looking at the inside of a ship. One end of the room held a large fieldstone fireplace with a deer head above it, and a grouping of leather couches facing it. In the middle of the room was a cherry table that could easily seat twelve and against a 'log' wall was a bar. Light poured into the room from floor- to- ceiling windows that looked out onto a pond.

"Must be nice," I said. I'm not a fan of this faux rusticity, but I had to admire the workmanship, especially the twig art that decorated the narrow balcony circling the room at the second story level.

"Come on," Janet said. "No time to gawk. We have work to do."

I followed her back to the car and, for the next twenty minutes I helped carry things to the kitchen, and then took appetizers in plastic containers, napkins, small plates and glasses from the box and put them on the kitchen table. Tim was busy setting up his bar in the living room.

Janet was looking at the plastic containers piled on the table. "I hope I've made enough food. Mr. Lincoln said he expected close to eighty people."

"Mr. Lincoln? George Lincoln?"

"Uh huh." Janet looked at me. "Do you know him?"

"I've only met him once. I need to tell you Janet..."

"Not now, Drew. Tell me later." She looked out through the open door to the parking lot. "Where the hell is Marcy. I told her to be here at three-thirty."

As if on cue, a car pulled into the parking lot and a young woman got out. She was wearing a voluminous white blouse and dark pants, and it was only when she turned sideways to say good-bye to the driver, that I saw she was very pregnant. She moved toward the kitchen. "Sorry," she said. "My boyfriend needs the car for his job. I told him I had to be here at three-thirty, but he was late getting back." She looked at Janet. "I'm here though."

"Good," Janet said. "You sure you can do this?"

The girl nodded. Janet pointed to the appetizers still in their plastic containers. "The crab appetizers, Southwestern egg rolls, turkey meatballs and stuffed mushrooms go into a warm oven," she said, pointing to the stove. "When those are hot, arrange them on platters and take them around. We can put the Artichoke dip, and the Guacamole out now with plenty of chips. The party nuts can go in dishes too." She opened a cupboard. "He was going to leave me some small serving bowls," she said, pushing dishes around. A box of medication fell out of the cupboard and a single green tablet fell from the box onto the floor.

"Oh hell," Janet said.

"I'll take care of it," I said. I put the medication box back on the shelf, and then seeing the errant pill, I tucked it into a napkin and stuffed it in my pocket. I'd return it later, when I had time. I filled one bowl with dip and another with chips. I put out the nuts, the chips and dips and then scurried back to the kitchen to start heating the appetizers. Janet said, "Just heat them up as you need them. That way they won't be forgotten and burned."

I could see people coming into the parking lot through the open door, and then there was the noise of chatter in the living room.

"Get to work," Janet said.

I took the appetizers from the oven, arranged them on a tray and headed to the living room. I could see George Lincoln holding forth at one end of the big room. The place was filling up and a line for drinks had formed at the bar. Beyond the floor-to-ceiling windows, the sun was shining on the pond.

"He's going to build houses all along here," one woman was saying to another, as I walked up to her with my tray. "Juniper Pond will be ruined."

"The cheapest house will be in the four hundred thousands," the second woman said. She chose an appetizer. "That's what this party is about, to try and sell properties."

"Where is his wife?" the first woman asked. She was hesitating between the eggrolls and the bacon-and blue-cheese filled mushrooms.

"She never comes with him," the second woman said, leaning toward her friend. "He used to be here only sporadically, but this summer he's been here all the time."

"Have you seen her picture?" the first woman said. She pointed to an area just to the left of the kitchen. "She's had a lot of work done."

The second woman turned to look at me for the first time. "You're the new art teacher, aren't you?"

I nodded.

"Miss Morgan, right?"

I nodded again, and since the woman didn't have anything else to ask, I moved on.

The place was filling up and getting noisier. I recognized Helen Limbeck, the psychiatrist, Mary Ellen Canson, my old boss at Adirondack Made, Jay Johnson, the principal of the school and Jud Weinstein. I moved around the group. When I got to Jud, I said. "What are you doing here?"

"The newspaper wants an article about this housing project." He pointed out a group of men standing talking near the bar. "Lincoln thinks he can sway the local politicians," He took four appetizers and put them on a plate. "Plus the guy likes to see himself in the paper."

"Have you learned anything else about Sara?"

He shook his head. "You?"

I leaned in closer. "They found Celestina's body in the woods. I'm surprised you didn't hear about it."

"Did you get pictures?"

"Sorry, no." Janet was watching me from the doorway to the kitchen. "Got to go, Jud. I'll call you."

I circulated around, avoiding George Lincoln. He seemed more interested in talking to the people around him than eating anyway. When my tray was empty, I headed back to the kitchen. As I got close to the door, I could see Marcy ahead of me. Suddenly she started to wobble, almost spilling her tray.

"Come on," I said, grabbing the empty tray, and pushing her through the kitchen door.

"What's going on?" I asked when we had reached the kitchen.

"I felt dizzy," she said. "I'll be better in a minute."

I was putting appetizers on a tray and pushing a new tray into the oven. Marcy had sunk into a seat.

"When did you eat last?" I asked.

She looked down at the table. "My boyfriend gets paid today and then we're going shopping. For sure we'll have enough then."

I grabbed two egg rolls and three mushrooms and set them down in front of her. "Eat, Marcy. You can't starve your baby."

"What's going on here?" It was George Lincoln standing in the doorway. "Why aren't you out there serving?

"We're just heating up the food, sir." Marcy said.

"And eating it? I don't pay you girls to eat my food. I pay you to wait on my guests."

"It fell on the floor," I lied. "I didn't think it should be served."

He moved closer and stared at me. "You're Drew Morgan. That woman from the mall. "

I nodded. I could smell the appetizers coming up to temperature and I reached down and pulled them out, putting the tray on the counter.

George Lincoln was still watching me. Finally he said, "Janet should have talked to me. I would not have hired you." When I said nothing, he barked. "Get to work, now."

"What a bastard," Marcy said when he'd left.

I was putting appetizers on trays for both of us. "How do you feel?" I asked.

"Better."

I handed her a tray. "We should go earn our pay."

On the way back to the living room, I stopped momentarily before the portrait of George and his wife. She wore a pale, strapless dress and expensive-looking jewelry. She didn't look happy. Something about the picture was familiar, but I couldn't think what it was.

George Lincoln had moved to a podium set up in a corner of the room. "Ladies and gentlemen," he began. "I am so glad you've all been able to come today. I wanted you to see first hand the quality that Lincoln Homes puts into their properties, and which will be put into the homes that I will be building here on Juniper Pond." He flicked on the large flat-screen TV that hung on the wall. The lights were dimmed and a carefully scripted ad for Lincoln Homes began.

"I come to this pond every summer to fish," a man behind me said. "I'll be damned if he's going to make it off limits."

"He's convinced the town council," a second man said. "All they see are jobs."

"Those jobs are finished once the project is done."

"They won't even hire local builders. He's promising jobs, but they won't be our jobs."

The film droned on. On the pond outside, two loons rested on the surface of the water and a flock of geese flew across the bright sky, things that would be no more once the homes were built. Instead there would be jet skis, motor boats, and noisy parties at docks, and maybe even a helipad to bring millionaires from their penthouses in New York City to these quiet woods. The film ended, and while George took a few questions, I looked around at the faces. Many people looked unhappy, not the reaction George had hoped for I'm sure. The questions ended; people finished eating and drinking, got their coats and jackets, and went home.

When the room was empty, I could see Janet in earnest conversation with George Lincoln. He was talking loudly, and Janet was shaking her head, upset.

"I have a reputation to uphold," George was saying. "Have you seen this house? It is luxurious, impeccable. How can I sell people on this lifestyle when you have a server waddling around like a fat little pig, and eating the food I paid for?"

"I will talk to her," Janet said. "I promise it won't happen again."

"And another thing. That woman, Drew Morgan. Do you know what she does for a living? She cleans toilets. Why would I want a woman who has come directly from cleaning shit out of toilets to be serving in my house? She's not even clean."

I didn't hear Janet's reply. I went to the sink and washed my hands and then started to scrape uneaten crab dip from a bowl into one of the plastic containers. I looked at Marcy who was emptying chips into a zip-lock bag, and putting uneaten appetizers into plastic boxes. Tim, the bartender, was putting unopened bottles of wine into cardboard boxes. Janet came into the kitchen.

"He's not paying us," she said.

"Not paying us?" Marcy echoed. She sat down suddenly. "Why not?"

Janet looked at me. "He felt that he should have had control over who I hired for this party. I told him that this is my company and I make that decision, but he was adamant." She looked at Marcy. "He doesn't like fat women as waitresses. He says it spoils the image."

"She's pregnant," I said. "Let me go talk to him. She needs the money. We all do. And…" I continued, "I didn't come here directly from cleaning rooms at the motel. I don't have that job any more."

"He didn't like my hiring you, Drew. Apparently he has met you before," Janet said. She looked at the bowls of chips sitting on the table and the unopened bottles of wine. "Luckily he paid me for the food when we made the arrangements. But he said if I want the rest of my money, I can go ahead and sue him." Tears were running down her cheeks as she handed the uneaten appetizers in plastic boxes to Marcy. "I am so sorry," she said.

Tim reached into his pocket and took out a wad of cash. "I made about a hundred in tips today," he said, peeling off two twenties and handing them to Marcy. "You need them more than I do."

He looked at me, but I held up my hand. "I'm good. Thank you Tim."

Janet had carried the dirty serving platters, and bowls to the sink and was starting to wash. "I took this job because I thought it would be good for business," she said. "He's a rich guy; he knows a lot of people in the area. Someone told me that he sometimes stiffs his workers, but I thought it was just a rumor."

"We should leave this mess," I said. "Let him deal with it himself."

She turned toward me. "You mean let his maid deal with it. These are my platters anyway."

I heard a noise and looked up to see a tall, lanky young man in the doorway.

"My boyfriend," Marcy said. She went with him to the parking lot and I watched a tearful, angry conversation between the two of them. Marcy pulled the cash out of her pocket and showed it to him; the boy put his arm around her shoulder.

"Don't forget your food," Janet called, running out with the leftovers. The young man nodded, took the containers, and putting his hand in Marcy's the two walked to the car.

"What do we do with this?" I asked, hefting a filled garbage bag.

"There's a trash bin behind the house," she said. "Come on, I'll show you." I followed her in silence to the back of the house where the trash bin stood. Between the house and the three-car garage was a browning lawn, a garage and, behind the garage tucked close to the fence, a small shed. Two of the garage doors were open, revealing a Mercedes and a motorcycle. If I'd been sixteen and had plenty of time, I would have keyed George Lincoln's Mercedes, scattered trash over his lawn, poured sugar into the gas tank of his motorcycle, egged his two-story windows, smeared shit around his marble bathroom, and carved graffiti onto the top of his four-thousand-dollar cherry table. But I wasn't sixteen and none of it would have made any difference.

There was a thumping noise from the shed. I was sure it was a dog penned up in there. If there is anything that makes me angrier than being stiffed for work I've done, it is people who mistreat their animals. It wouldn't take much for me to go to the shed, release the dog and take him home, but it would be impossible to do now because Janet had come into the yard and was saying, "Come on, Drew. We're done here. Let's go home."

I went home, poured myself a soda and sat on the couch beside Lilli, trying to tamp down the anger I still felt. I didn't know what George Lincoln had gained this afternoon. Throwing a big party wasn't going to make people like him and might not even get his project approved. Even though he was spreading his money around the community, he was still a stranger, and for some, an unwelcome one.

I needed to move and find closure for my anger, so I put on Lilli's leash and we headed out for a walk. I still had not made a decision about whether to return to New York City and find work there, but I needed to do something because my reserve of available funds was running low. The sun was going down, dusting the sky with wide swatches of vermillion and orange and the lights from the houses dotting the edge of the lake glowed against the dark. I would hate to leave this community. If there were any way I could keep myself going financially I would stay.

My phone rang. It was Jud.

"Some party, eh?" he said.

"The dance for the search and rescue dogs was better."

"Someone told me that money can't buy you love."

"He refused to pay us, Jud. He said Marcy, who's pregnant, was a fat little pig and he doesn't like me."

"I could put that in my article about the party. Not everyone loves him you know."

"Sure, whatever you can do." I went on to tell him about finding Celestina's body. "You should talk to the police," I said. "They can give you the details."

"Do you know how she died?"

"No. Sara was strangled, but I couldn't tell how Celestina was killed."

"She disappeared around August 21 and it's now late September. Was she in the woods all this time?"

"I've no idea, Jud. Listen, I've got to go."

"Sure. Thanks for the information, Drew."

When I returned home, I changed out of the dark pants and blouse I'd worn earlier and put them into the laundry basket. As I touched the pants, I felt something in the pocket. The pill. I'd forgotten all about the pill that had fallen onto the floor when Janet was looking for bowls, and which I'd tucked into my pocket.

Now, I had no chance to return it. Unwrapping the napkin, I studied the pill. It was oblong and light green. I tried to remember the name of the drug that had been on the box, but I'm not a pharmacist, so it wouldn't have made any difference. Tomorrow was Saturday, maybe I could pay a visit to the local CVS.

It was still early evening, and I needed something to take my mind off the anger that still boiled inside. I called Matt's number but it went to voicemail. Damn. It would be a movie on Netflix and a pint of Ben & Jerry's for supper.

Chapter Thirty-One

The CVS pharmacy sat in a small shopping mall not far from my house. Like the previous day, this one was glorious, and I was a little sorry that I was wasting it driving to the drug store. Nevertheless I was in luck because I was the only one in line and the druggist, a youngish man with bright red hair and horn-rimmed glasses, agreed to come out from behind his counter to talk with me.

I handed him the pill. "I found this in my brother's bedroom," I said. "I think he's messing around with something illegal. Can you tell me what it is?"

"Rohypnol," the druggist said. "It is illegal, but you can get it by mail. Sometimes called Forget-Me-Pills, Mexican Valium, Roaches, Wolfies. It's a date-rape drug."

"Let me show you something," he said, leaving his post behind the counter and coming back a few minutes later with a glass of water. He set the glass down in front of me and then dropped the pill into the glass. "When these pills were first manufactured, they were white and colorless in water, but the FDA put a colorant in them." I watched as the water in the glass turned blue.

"Rohypnol can still be put in a drink and no one will notice the color, especially if the drink has a color of its own."

"What exactly does it do?"

"It impairs judgment, reduces inhibitions and, with alcohol, it can produce exaggerated intoxication. Cocaine addicts sometimes use it to relieve the irritability and agitation from cocaine binges. But the drug is most often used to incapacitate women and target them for sex. They don't remember what happened. If your brother has any more of this, I would get rid of it. It's bad stuff."

As I drove back to the apartment, my mind was in a whirl. George Lincoln could be a cocaine addict, though I'd not been in his bathroom or his bedroom where I might find needles. If he weren't an addict, but was using the drug to assault women, it might be in the kitchen because he was using it in a drink.

There was something else about George tickling the back of my mind. Something not fully formed that had to do with the picture of his wife I'd seen in the house. I tried to think what it was but nothing was working. When I got back to the apartment and started back up the stairs, I could see that Lilli was reluctant to follow. If she could have spoken, she would have said. "Wait a minute. You're going to spend the day in there. It's a great day. Why aren't we out for a walk?"

But I needed to follow a thought. I got to my computer and pulled up the website for Lincoln Properties and slid through half a dozen pictures of properties before I remembered his "About George" pages. I flipped through the pictures quickly, until I came to George Lincoln standing beside his wife. I studied the picture of Mrs. Lincoln, the same one that had been in the house. It wasn't the woman herself I was studying, it was what she was wearing. It wasn't the dress. It was the necklace. I printed the picture, and then I went back to the photos I had saved from Sara's phone. It was hard to look at the nudes. She was so young and pretty and I couldn't see that beauty without remembering the body in the woods. And then I found it, Sara on her knees, her breasts hanging down, her head lifted, wearing a jeweled necklace. The same necklace that Mrs. George Lincoln was wearing in her photo.

This was a link, but was it enough? George Lincoln was a big benefactor in the town. Would the police take me seriously? I picked up the phone and dialed Matt's number, but it went to voicemail again. Where the hell was he?

"Matt, this is Drew. I was at George Lincoln's house yesterday waitressing for a party. There was a drug in his kitchen cupboard called Rohypnol. I checked it out with a pharmacist and it's a date-rape drug. Something bothered me about the picture of his wife so when I got home, I looked at the nude photos of Sara from her phone. Sara is wearing a necklace that is identical to the one George's wife is wearing in a picture on his web site. The Rohypnol and the necklace are a link, aren't they? Please call me, Matt. I need to talk to you. The other thing is that I'm sure he's got a dog locked in a wooden shed behind the house. I'm going to go and rescue it."

I don't know why I told him about the dog. I hadn't, until that moment decided that I would try and save the animal. If Lincoln had killed Sara, I couldn't save her, and it was possible there wouldn't even be enough evidence to convict him. The only thing I could do was to try to save an animal.

But I needed to do it at night.

Chapter Thirty-Two

The world is always different at night. Places that you know so well, that you could find your way around without thinking, become alien without light. I had decided for this little adventure that I would leave Lilli at home, but I loaded up a backpack with a flashlight, crowbar, a bag of dog food and water. I would somehow have to release the dog from its chains, and so I put a pair of pliers into the pack. I dressed in dark pants, a long sleeved dark shirt, and hiking boots, then I put a dark ski cap on my head. Ninja warrior? I had no Shuriken, Kama or Kusarigama. My wits would have to do.

I drove up to the house and parked along the road. The parking lot where I'd put my car yesterday had a high metal fence closing it off, but tonight the fence was locked. Nevertheless, I had what I thought were two sources of good luck. There were no lights coming from inside the house, which might mean that George Lincoln wasn't at home, and there was a big, bright full moon. I looked at the house, trying to assess how I could get in. To the left was the locked parking area and to the right, and all around the house, was a tall chain-link fence. As I walked up to the fence, a motion-sensor light flashed on, bathing the place with light. Luckily for me, this side of the house had only one window, so even though there was light outside, nothing stirred. Still I waited, watching for someone inside, but nothing happened. Creeping close to the edge of the fence, I saw a tiny, narrow opening between the edge of the fence, and the house, a gap just large enough for me to squeeze through. I had to be careful; if I weren't, everything would be bathed in light again. Squeezing through the gap and pushing myself against the fence I crept along the edge of the lawn, trying to stay out of the range of the lights. The dirt at the base of the fence was littered with stones and once I fell, hitting my knee and crying out. I waited, not breathing, but no lights came on and I crept forward. I was now close to the garage. All of the stalls were wide open, the Mercedes in one, the motorcycle in the second and in the third, what looked like a red Volvo. I fished out my cell phone and shone the light on the car. Pennsylvania plates. This must be Sara's car. I snapped a picture, and had just moved away, when a light flicked on in the kitchen and George Lincoln's figure was silhouetted in the door. "Who's there?" he called.

I ducked into the garage. I had no weapon and I was clearly trespassing and if George Lincoln had killed Sara, he wouldn't hesitate to kill me. George moved out into the yard, the lights clicking on, bathing the area in light.

"Who's there," he called again. Maybe there would be a dog, like Darryl Boxer's Rottweiler that would lunge forward, growling and snapping. I waited, watching George move toward me in the light, then change his mind and start back toward the house. He disappeared into the house and the yard lights went out.

I moved into the garage and snapped another picture of the Volvo. Would this be enough to get the police involved? I hoped so.

Suddenly there was a noise behind me, and before I could turn, I felt something around my neck.

"I thought I'd had enough of you, yesterday, Miss Morgan. Decided to do a little sightseeing?" George Lincoln asked.

The cord around my neck was being pulled tighter and I was gasping for breath. I kicked out, trying to make contact, but the thing choking off my wind didn't let up. I reached toward the cord, trying to claw it away, but there was still no change. I was starting to see stars, losing strength. Suddenly I thought of my backpack, which I'd removed when I squeezed through the fence and which I held in my hand. The backpack was heavy, and I didn't know if I had the strength to swing it behind me. But I had to try. With every bit of power I had, I swung the backpack and heard it hit with a thump.

"Damn," George said. The cord loosened and I pulled it off, moving away quickly. We were in the middle of the yard, still in bright light. I looked around. The only place I could hide was the garage. I ducked into a stall.

I could hear him behind me, breathing heavily. There was only a narrow space between the edge of the garage and the Mercedes, but I squeezed past it, praying that there was a back door. There was none. George was now directly behind me. I crossed behind the front of the Mercedes and ran down the other side, but George doubled back to meet me at the entrance.

We were face to face. With all my strength, I swung the backpack again, hitting him square in the face. He staggered and fell and I ran. I was now between the chain link fence and the shed, where I could hear something moving around inside. It was dark back here, but I wasn't sure now that I could rescue an animal and then race back to the front of the house, before George caught up with me. What had I been thinking when I decided to take this on?

I could hear heavy breathing and I moved away. There were trees on the other side of the fence, blocking out the moonlight. I stepped further back, and felt someone behind me."Gotcha," George said.

He had me by the back of my jacket. I pulled forward, felt fabric rip, was temporarily free but on the ground and he was pulling me backward by my legs. I still had the backpack, but now it was being wrestled from my hands. I heard it thump against the side of the shed as George threw it. I struggled, but George was stronger. Pulling me up, he muscled my arms behind me as he began marching me toward the shed. I kicked backward, trying to connect. Somehow he'd got the cord around my neck again and was pulling on it, and I realized that if I struggled harder, I would be strangled.

We had reached the shed, which was padlocked. George released me and started undoing the lock. I sprinted toward the fence, but I was too slow, and when he caught up with me, I had nothing to strike him with. Grabbing me by the arm he marched me toward the door of the shed, opened it and threw me in.

The shed was pitch black and the smell of urine made my eyes water. God damn this man. I had lost my backpack with the dog food, flashlight, and crowbar and now I was locked inside a shed with what might be a vicious dog. Something moved in the corner. Carefully I pulled out my phone and aimed the light toward the sound. There, crouched against the wall was a girl.

Chapter Thirty-Three

The girl, who was hunched against the wall of the shed, was no more than twelve. Her hair was stringy and unwashed, there were tear streaks running down her dirty face and she was dressed in a stained T-shirt and jeans. Her feet were bare.

"Where's Sara?" the girl asked. Her voice was rusty from disuse and I looked around for water but there was none. Only a metal dish with food, around which flies buzzed.

"Are you her sister?"

The girl shook her head.

"But you came up from Pennsylvania with her."

The girl nodded. This was going to take time.

"How long have you been here?"

"Weeks and weeks," she said.

I pointed to the dish. "Is this what he feeds you?"

She nodded. "Only I don't eat it, 'cause he puts drugs in there. That's what happened to Sara. He drugged her food and then he took her outside to do things to her. When she came back, she couldn't remember nothin' and she would sleep for the whole day."

"If you don't eat, how do you stay alive?"

She shrugged. "I eat a little bit ever once in a while, but I never eat all the food."

"What's your name, sweetie?"

"Ranji. Ranji Singh." She had started to cry, deep wrenching sobs. "I miss my mom," she said.

"Do your parents know where you are?"

A shake of the head. She had bent her head toward her knees, her whole thin body shaking as she cried. I sat beside her on the filthy mattress and put my arms around her.

"I shouldn't have run away," she said between sobs, "but my cousin Bukka, he started coming into my room at night and you know, wanting to mess with me."

"Did you tell your parents?"

"They didn't believe me. Bukka is a boy, and I'm only a girl. I tried to keep him out, but I didn't have a lock."

"How did you meet Sara Kyzinski?"

"She came to do makeup at our school. Our teacher, Miss Leland, arranged it as a special treat. Then me and Sara began e-mailing and texting each other. She was mad at her dad, and I was mad at my parents, and she said she knew this guy who would help us buy a car and find a place to live, so we came up here."

"And you both moved into the cabin in the woods."

She nodded. "It got old after a while. Sara wanted to go to New York City, and I was starting to miss my folks. Sara drove me to the bus station and I got on with my suitcase." She pointed to a dark lump in the corner of the bed. "It's still here."

"How did you end up here?"

"This guy gets on the bus and drags me off. He says he don't want Sara to run away again. He throws Sara and me into this shed, and then he starts putting things in Sara's food that made her sleepy."

As Ranji talked, I was looking around the shed, plotting a way to get out. George Lincoln might leave us here to starve for days, or he might return in fifteen minutes to kill me. But I had already been lost in the woods and wandered around for days. If that hadn't killed me, a scumbag like George wouldn't do it either.

I took my cell phone and dialed Matt's number but it went to voicemail. It was no use. I was wasting the battery and I needed the phone for light. Holding it up, I made an assessment of the shed. The boards making up the walls looked worn, as though someone had taken what was already old and slapped something together as a place to store materials. I picked up the metal food dish and dumped the fly-covered mess in a corner.

"You didn't tell me about Sara," Ranji said. "Where is she?"

She didn't know. Of course not. She'd been here, cut off from everything for weeks. "She died," I said.

Ranji started to cry again. "I told her not to do it. She tried to run away, twice. The first time she got over the fence before he caught her. Then he said he'd put animal traps in the woods and no one would get past them. When she didn't come back the second time, I thought she'd got away."

I sat down on the mat and hugged her. "Thank you for telling me about the traps," I said. "But don't worry, we are getting out of here."

"He's got a gun," Ranji said. "I saw it when he brought Sara back the first time."

I stood up, picked up the metal dish and wedged the edge between a crack in the boards that made up the walls. I could feel the walls give very slightly, but the dish was thin and would probably break before I pulled away a board. With the plate still in my hand, I walked over to the door where the hinges were old and rusty. I might have better luck, prying out the screws. I put the dish under the edge of a hinge and gently levered it. The hinge moved.

"What are you doing?" Ranji asked.

"Getting us out."

"You can't do that. If we mess with his stuff, he will kill us."

Lincoln would kill us even if we sat here and did nothing. I was not going to let that happen without a fight. I worked on a hinge for about twenty minutes, levering it up until the rusty screws began to pop out. It was tough work and the trick in taking off a hinge is that you do it little by little. If you take all the screws out of the top hinge, the door sags, making it hard to remove the bottom hinge, so I worked carefully between the upper and lower hinges. When all the hinges were loose but not removed, I returned to where Ranji was and sat down beside her.

"Let's see what's in your suitcase?"

"Not much," she said. She pulled the suitcase toward me. I turned on the cell phone and handed it to the child. "Hold this up," I said. "I want to look inside."

The suitcase held mostly clothing, but there were also a hair curler, hair spray, makeup, a pair of shoes, and a flashlight.

I held up the flashlight. "Does this still work?"

Ranji shook her head. I flicked the switch, the light glowed weakly. Hopefully there was still enough juice for what I needed. I unscrewed the top, tipped out the two double A batteries, and put them in my pocket.

I turned back to the suitcase, pulling out the hairspray and a pair of wool socks. I needed something else and then I remembered the food. It had been wrapped in aluminum foil. I found where I'd thrown the remains of the meal into the corner and tore a strip from the edge of the foil. I smoothed it out against my knee.

"What are you doing?"

"Making a fire," I said. "This past summer I got lost in the woods and had no way to stay warm, so after I was rescued I decided I would learn to make fire so the next time it happened I could stay warm."

"You rub two sticks together," Ranji said.

"There are easier ways." I looked at the rough wood of the walls beside me, and then picked up the metal food dish. The edge had been bent by the effort of pulling screws from the hinges. Grabbing the plate by both edges I began to work it quickly back and forth, bending it first one way and then the other until it snapped in half, leaving a nice, rough, metal edge."

"He's not going to like this," Ranji said.

I moved closer and put my arms around her. "One of the things I have learned is that you always have to try. When you're in a tough situation, you can't give up. If you give up, someone has beaten you. I think George Lincoln killed Sara and he will kill

231

us if we let him. But we aren't going to let him. I have a plan to get us out of here. It's gonna' be dangerous and a little bit scary, but I think we can do it. Can you work with me on this?"

Her body was still trembling, but she looked at me with her tear-stained face and nodded.

"Now," I said. "I want you to stand up and walk around." The shed was so small, there was hardly room to stand, let alone walk. "Later, I'm going to tell you to run, and you need to run as fast as you can. Then you'll have to climb a fence. You think you can do that?"

She nodded again. "What about the traps?" she asked. "Aren't they still there?"

"I think so," I said, remembering Sara's amputated foot. He had found her in the field, killed her and cut off her foot so no one would know about the traps. "But we'll worry about those things when we get to them."

I turned to the wall of the shed and began scraping away slivers of wood with the sharp edge of the metal dish until finally I had a small pile of sticks that fire builders call a 'nest.' I held up a wool sock. "Can I use this?" I asked.

She nodded and while she provided the light from my phone, I unraveled a bit of the wool and laid the strands on top of the nest. I cut a longer shard of wood from the wall, and put it beside the nest, and beside that, I put the hairspray. Then I took the rectangular strip of aluminum foil, and wrapped one end around the negative pole of the battery, leaving the other end dangling free. I tucked another strip of the foil into my pocket, along with the second battery. This would be my back-up. I put the nest of wood shavings and wool, the long piece of wood, the battery with its dangling foil and the hairspray carefully onto the broken metal dish. I would have to perform a tricky maneuver in the dark, and I wasn't sure if it would work, but I had to try.

I looked over at Ranji, in her T-shirt and bare feet. Scrambling through the suitcase again, I pulled out a long sleeved shirt, another pair of socks and sneakers. There was nothing else I could give her, except courage. That she would have to find on her own.

After she had dressed she stood up, head bowed and began saying something softly in a language I didn't understand.

"It is a good luck chant," she said. "Asking for guidance and protection." I moved to put my arms around her. I loved the brave heart of this child who had endured so much. We would need every bit of courage we could summon, and a little bit of luck, but we would try.

It was still quiet outside and I had no idea what George Lincoln was doing. It might have been better to do this in daytime, when we could better make out the traps in the woods ahead, but darkness would give us cover. We needed to do it now.

"Are you ready?" I asked. She nodded. I turned on the phone so she would have light, then I went to the door and pulled the screws out of the hinges. The door sagged but stayed where it was. I pushed hard against the door and with a loud squeak it started to move. I needed to work fast in case George came running. I pushed again and when the opening was large enough, I pushed Ranji out, reaching back to retrieve the metal dish with its weapons.

I followed Ranji to the fence and boosted her up. She was still weak from her ordeal as a prisoner, but she was willing. I watched as she climbed slowly up the fence, reached the top and dropped down to the other side.

"You will come, won't you?" she said.

"I will come. Wait for me in the woods. Use the light from the phone to find your way."

I was heavier and older than Ranji so it would take me a few minutes more to get myself over the fence. But, because there were no motion-sensor lights out here, I would have the protection of darkness and if George came for me, I had a weapon. I could have easily climbed the fence now, but even as I hesitated, the kitchen light switched on, and the figure of George came into the yard and started across the brightly lit lawn. Carefully, my heart beating and my palms sweaty I made my way to where I'd put my weapons. It was pitch black and it took me a minute to find the stuff. Taking up the battery, I watched as George walked toward me until he was beyond the pool of light, coming into the dark. Still watching him, I wrapped the loose end of the foil around the positive pole of the battery. The battery sparked. I dropped it into the nest and the nest flared. George was only a few yards away. I needed to wait until he was closer, but I still had the cover of dark. Reaching down, I lit a long stick from the burning nest, and picked up the hair spray, so I had fire in one hand, and the accelerant in the other. Then I moved toward George.

"God damn it, what's going on," he said.

I stepped up so we were only a foot apart. Squeezing the button on the hairspray, I lit it with my 'match' and flame shot out directly into George's face

"Jesus Christ," he yelled. He was writhing on the ground, trying to rub out the fire against the grass. I dropped the hairspray into the nest and sprinted for the fence.

Chapter Thirty-Four

Ranji was waiting for me in the woods, holding the cell phone whose battery was rapidly dying. "Someone called you," she said. "But I didn't answer it."

I nodded, hoping it was Matt, but even as I looked at the screen, the phone went black. We were in the woods, where moonlight couldn't reach us and there were animal traps all around, waiting to dig into the flesh of our ankles

"Be careful," Ranji said. She had reached back to pick up a stick to help her walk, when suddenly I heard a huge boom and saw the lights from a fire. "Good," I said aloud. I hoped the hairspray had exploded, setting the shed and the grass around it on fire. I wanted the fire to spread to the garage and the house. I wanted it to consume George Lincoln, lying unconscious on the ground.

But I had no such luck. Suddenly something whizzed by me and landed with a thunk in the tree immediately to my right.

"It's him," Ranji said. "He's shooting us."

We started walking faster, but with the limited light of the moon, it was hard to see what was underfoot. The undergrowth was rooted and rocky and twice I stumbled, willing myself not to tumble into an animal trap. We were now on a woods road, probably the Juniper Pond road that circled the hill and ended at the dump where we'd found Sara's body. A bullet whizzed by and I could hear George behind us cursing us as he ran.

I pulled us toward the edge of the road and we sat. We needed a better plan, but I had no idea what it was. Suddenly Ranji pointed. There just ahead of us was a light, dim and bobbing, as though someone were walking through the woods with a lantern. We stood up and the light began to move. It was snaking a path along the road, leading us forward.

"Is this safe?" Ranji asked.

"I'm not sure," I said. I'd heard of phantom lights that appear without explanation, but I'd never experienced anything that seemed as deliberate as this was. We followed the light along the road. I couldn't hear George any more, but that didn't mean we were out of danger. He could simply have stopped to reload his gun. Suddenly I heard a groan and a cry for help.

"Maybe he stepped into one of his own traps," I said.

The light moved along the road, guiding us to the edge of a grassy slope, the same sloping field which Matt, Jim and I had hiked up to find Sara. In the open field, with the moonlight shining down, it was easier to see where we were walking, but I could still see the light bobbing ahead of us, leading us to safety. As we neared the road, I heard sirens and saw police cars careening past their lights blazing. We were going to make it.

Chapter Thirty-Five

We staggered toward the road, now empty of cars. Ranji was trembling with cold and fatigue and I realized we would need to get her to a hospital soon because her strength was almost gone.

"Come on, Sweetie. Just a little farther. We're almost there," I said. It was possible that George Lincoln was still behind us, trying to shoot at us, but I hadn't heard any gunshots in a while. I hoped that the police had found a way into the house and were now swarming over the grassy lawn, peering into the shed, seeing the ruined door and the scorched grass around the nest and the exploded remains of the hair spray can. Maybe they would find him, caught in one of his own traps in the wood. Maybe they were, even now, looking for us and all we had to do was sit and wait.

I heard the siren before I saw the car, but it sped by on the opposite side of the road, before I had time to stand and flag it down. I barely had time before the next one came down the road, but this time I staggered to the edge and stepped out directly into the path. I had nothing else to make myself visible. The car made a fast U-turn, and careened to a stop, its lights still flashing.

I watched as the cop stepped out of the car. He was wearing his flack vest and had an enormous flashlight, which as he walked closer, he played over my face.

"Do you know you can get killed like that?" he said. "Who the hell are you?"

"Drew Morgan. You might be looking for me."

"Jesus. What are you doing here?"

Instead of answering, I struggled to the side of the road where Ranji sat and pulled her to her feet. "This is Ranji Singh. She is the girl who was in the shed."

"Christ," he said again. "We've got half a dozen cops out looking for you. I've got to call this in." He gestured toward the car. "Sit inside where it's warm."

We moved to the back seat of the car and half listened to the cop talking on the phone. I wanted to tell him that we needed an ambulance, but he seemed to have that under control. Ranji was still shaking. The stress of running through the woods being chased by a man with a gun was taking its toll. I had not been a prisoner in a shed for months, so I was in better shape, but I was pretty stressed myself.

I thought how lucky I had been. Somehow Matt had gotten the message about George Lincoln and sent the Mounties out to save me. I'd been able to outwit George and we'd made it across a landmine of traps in the dark, but it could all have ended very differently. Someone had been watching out for us.

At that moment, a police car appeared behind us and pulled up, its headlights shining through the rear window. The back door to the car opened and Matt stood there.

"Oh God, Drew," he said.

I squeezed myself out of the car and walked into his embrace. "I was away at a conference," he said. "Or I would have talked you out of what you decided to do."

He pushed me away, still hanging on to my shoulders. "Do you know that you are one crazy woman? He could have shot you."

"I know. He was shooting at us while we were running away."

"Us?"

"Us." I pulled Matt toward the open door of the car where Ranji had pushed herself against the far corner. "Meet Ranji Singh. She is the girl who was in the shed. The girl George was holding prisoner."

"We saw the shed door. It was still padlocked. Did you take those hinges off?"

I nodded.

"And the explosive hair spray? That was your idea?"

I nodded.

I leaned toward him. "She needs to get to the hospital, Matt. She's been in that shed for a while, not eating the food because it was drugged. I don't know what else he did to her."

"Poor kid," Matt said. He stepped away from the car and began talking to the police officer, the gist of their conversation being the girl. But the cop had already called for an ambulance because a few minutes later, one came roaring up the road, made a skillful U-turn, and parked. Then they got Ranji onto a gurney and into the ambulance. I said we would see her at the hospital.

Chapter Thirty-Six

"What in God's name made you go to that house?" Matt asked.

We were sitting in the cafeteria of the hospital. Ranji had been given a bed and the preliminary report on her condition was guarded but good. She was suffering from malnutrition, and exposure and had possibly been sexually assaulted, but no one was mentioning that. Her parents who lived in Philadelphia had been called.

"I didn't think it was dangerous. I was angry at George Lincoln because he refused to pay us and I was going to get back at him by stealing his dog."

"His dog?"

"I thought it was a dog in the shed. I heard it making noise when I took out the trash."

"How were you going to get the dog out from behind the fence once you rescued it?"

"I didn't think about that."

"Oh God, Drew. Oh God." He put his head in his hands, probably wondering how he'd ever got mixed up with a noodle-brain like me. Then he stood up, walked over to me and drew me into his arms. "Do you know you are both the bravest and the most insane woman I have ever met."

"Is that a good thing?"

"I'm not sure."

I leaned into his hug. "Sara's car is in George's garage. I saw it when he was chasing me around the yard. And he has some sort of date-rape drug in his cupboards. I told you that on the phone. And the necklace Sara is wearing in the nude photo belongs to George Lincoln's wife. She is wearing it in a photo on his website."

We were both quiet, feeling the comfort in each other's arms.

Matt disengaged himself and sat down, taking a sip of his coffee. "Did Sara and Ranji come from the same town?"

"I don't think so, but I think they came up to the Adirondacks together. Lorraine, the hairdresser at A Cut Above said that Darryl, Sara's friend, often came into the salon with his sister while Sara was working. Ranji was the sister."

"And no one noticed her?"

"I don't know. She was just someone's little sister. She wasn't in school, just hanging around in that cabin in the woods."

Matt took a sip of his coffee. "I'm sure George killed Celestina too. Was that because Celestina told you to look for the girl?"

"But Celestina was killed *after* Sara was found. If George was trying to keep Celestina from telling us where Sara's body was, why do it then?"

"Maybe Sara told Celestina who her killer was, and Celestina wanted to tell you."

"It could be. But I think it was more than that."

"What are you thinking?"

"When Sara told me to 'find the girl' she wasn't talking about herself. She wouldn't have said that because she was already dead, and it might not have mattered to her whether she was found or not. The girl Sara was talking about, the girl she wanted us to find, was Ranji who was still alive and being held hostage by George."

I took a sip of coffee. "When Celestina called me and said it was urgent that we talk, I think she might have known, through Sara, exactly where Ranji was. Somehow George found out that Celestina knew he had kidnapped Ranji and that's why she was killed."

We were interrupted by a doctor who'd apparently been looking for us. "The girl is awake and wants to talk with you," he said looking at me.

"Both of us?" I indicated Matt.

"Detective Weims is there. I'm sure it will be OK."

We walked up to Ranji's room which seemed to be crowded with people, though it was only Jim, a nurse, Dr. Turner, and now Matt and me. Ranji lay propped up against pillows, her face pale and with a tube connected from her arm to an IV. Beside her on a stand were water, orange juice and a covered dish of food.

"She's doing very well, considering what she's gone through," Dr. Turner said, looking at his young patient.

"When are my parents coming?" Ranji asked.

"They are on their way. We called them as soon as we could, but it will take them a while to get here from Philadelphia," Jim said.

"Can you tell us how you met Sara Kyzinski?" Jim asked
Ranji gently.

The girl licked her lips, and I reached for the water glass and
gently put the straw up to her lips.

"She was Molly B. The girl who did makeup. I knew her from
YouTube. My parents were real strict about makeup, and what I
wore. No short skirts or see-through blouses. I could only go to
parties where they knew the parents, and could only stay until
nine---that kind of thing." She licked her lips, and I gave her more
water.

"But I liked putting on makeup. It made me feel pretty. I
started to writing to Molly---Sara---on the internet."

"Using Snapchat."

She nodded. "My parents are real nosy. At first it was just, you
know, talk about what product you use, how do you get it so it
won't rub off. We talked about how hard it was to be the only kid
in the family, that kind of stuff. She was fighting with her dad and
I was---unhappy."

"Unhappy?"

"My cousin Bukka had come to live with us. He was older
than me---fifteen, and you know, the prince in the house. After a
few weeks he started coming into my room at night when I was in
bed. I told him no. I tried to push him away. I put a chair up
against the door, but it was hard to keep him out." She looked at
me. "I told you all about it."

"Did you talk to your parents?" Jim asked.

"I tried to, but they didn't believe me. Even though I was their daughter and he was just a cousin, they believed him over me."

"So what happened?"

"Sara and I decided to run away. One day when my parents were at work and my cousin was at school, I went home, grabbed my suitcase and took the bus to Philly. Sara had got money from this boy she knew, and bought an old Volvo. She was old enough to drive, so we drove up here. It was a long trip, but we made it."

"I'm surprised the police never found where you had gone." I said.

"Philadelphia is a big city and Sara's father didn't tell the cops she was missing until a few days after she'd left." Jim said. "Those few days can make all the difference in an investigation." He looked at Ranji. "Your parents have been looking for you for four months. They have been frantic."

"Is my cousin still there?"

"I don't know. I only talked to them briefly."

"Anyway," Ranji continued. "Sara's friend Darryl found us a house in the woods and that's where we stayed." She lay back on the pillows exhausted.

"We can come back later," Jim said, reaching forward and touching her hand. "When you've had some rest."

Ranji's eyes had closed, and we had begun to rise from our seats when she said. "Sara was tired of Saranac Lake. She wanted to make more money. I could go with her if I wanted to, but I really missed my mom and dad and I thought---I thought--that things would be different."

"You should get some sleep," Jim said.

She moved to sit up straighter and I adjusted a pillow behind her. "Sara drove me to the bus station and bought me a ticket. I waved good-bye. The bus was just starting and then it stopped. This man got on, tall with grey hair and said I should get off now, that Sara was in an accident. How could she be in an accident? I asked. I just saw her. But he said I had to get off, and when he got me to Sara's car, she was in the back seat, passed out. He pushed me inside and started driving, but when I asked where we were going he told me to shut up. Then he handed me a coke to drink, and when I woke up we were in the shed behind his house."

"Do you remember what day it was when you went to the bus?"

"July tenth. It was my mom's birthday, and I was gonna surprise her."

Ranji had been in the shed for three months. I thought of my own brief time in that airless space. It must have been terrifying. But then she had Sara to keep her company at least for part of that time.

"What happened after you went into the shed?" Jim asked.

"Could I have some water?"

I leaped up to get a glass and held the straw to her mouth so she could drink.

"Sara decided she was going to escape. She wanted me to come with her, but I was scared. She said once she got out, she'd find a way to get me out too. The man liked her more than he liked me and sometimes he would come and take her out of the shed for a while. When she came back she was sleepy, like she'd been drugged. He would just open the door, push her in and lock it behind her. One day I heard Sara and the man yelling outside the shed.When he didn't open the door and throw her in, I figured she had escaped, but that evening, she was back. The man said he was gonna put animal traps in the woods where she couldn't see them, and if she tried to escape again, she'd be caught."

"But she tried again?"

"I told her not to do it. I said he was a bad man that would kill her for sure. But she didn't listen. The next time she had a chance she ran. I never saw her again."

Jim was sitting with his head bent almost to his knees as though he were going to vomit on the floor. Matt was rubbing his hands on his legs as though trying to get rid of something nasty. All I could see was the image of Sara's body, bloated and dark with the foot cut off.

Ranji had put her head back down on the pillow and had closed her eyes. It was now close to one o'clock and all of us were emotionally exhausted. There was a knock on the door and then it opened. Two people came in; she was wearing a purple sari and he was in a dark suit. Ranji's parents.

"We need to go," Jim said, walking over to introduce himself to Ranji's father. Turning to me he said, "We'll talk later."

Chapter Thirty-Seven

George Lincoln was arraigned for the kidnapping, assault and murder of Sara Kyzinski and for the kidnapping and assault of Ranji Singh. In spite of his attempts to 'buy' the community there were plenty of people like Janet whom he'd cheated, and who were willing to testify against his character. It would take time for the prosecution to assemble a case, even though the evidence clearly showed him as guilty. The trial would be a media circus, but the judge was not going to move for a change of venue. Jud would certainly get his book and we all hoped that justice would be done.

On a cool early evening in late December, six people climbed Mount Arab in the growing dark, carrying the ashes of a beloved dog. The people were Matt and me, Jim, his wife, Penny and their two children. The dog whose ashes they carried was WhizBang. The six of us climbed the steps of the fire tower, and squeezed into the top watching the streaked purple sky spread across the horizon above the winking lights of Tupper Lake. Jim opened a window, and let the wind pull the ashes out into the bright evening air. "Go with grace, WhizBang," he said. We stood in silence, watching the light fade and the bits of WhizBang move into the air. WhizBang had loved the mountains, and it was fitting that his remains should be here, in the trees and the ground, the water and the air. Whiz had not only brought Jim back to sanity, he had mentored Hershey who had brought Matt back. A dog who had found his calling, not in herding sheep but in finding people was now gone.

In silence, we climbed down the stairs of the tower and switched on our headlamps. The last of the winter sun was staining the sky a deep red as we moved into the woods, thinking about a border collie's legacy.

We were in a line, Jim's wife ahead of me, Matt behind.

"What's the difference between a ghost and an angel?" I asked Matt.

"Is this a riddle? OK, I'll bite. What's the difference between a ghost and an angel?"

"It's not a riddle. I'm serious. I've been thinking about this a lot."

"I have no idea what the difference is. If you've been thinking about this, tell me."

I sighed. It would be hard but I was going to give it a try. "You know I first met Sara Kyzinski as a ghost. I was in the woods--- dying, and she came floating through. She wasn't trying to scare me, just get my attention."

"So not a ghost?"

"She was only a ghost that first time. In the next couple of weeks she kept turning up, first with Celestina and then in my dreams, always with the same message 'Find the girl.' She wasn't a specter in the woods any more, she was a spirit with a mission."

"I have to tell you that I don't believe in ghosts. Not even ones with a mission."

"When Ranji and I were running from George Lincoln, I didn't know how we would get out of the woods. It was dark. He'd planted the traps and was shooting at us, but there was this light, like someone walking in front of us with a lantern."

"A ghost?"

"Not a ghost, an angel. Someone who had worked hard to make sure that Ranji was found and when she was found, guiding us to safety. Sara was watching over us, making sure we were going to be safe."

"Maybe it wasn't Sara. Maybe it was your sister who led you out of the woods."

I'd assumed the spirit protecting us was Sara. I looked back at Matt trying to read the expression on his face.

"It's possible, isn't it?" he said. "It could have been Carley who led you through the woods. It could have been your sister trying to make sure you were safe."

I looked down at the path, steep and rocky and barely illuminated by my headlamp. In all the years I'd been mourning the loss of my sister, I hadn't thought of her watching over me. Making sure I was safe.

"Careful," Matt said. "It can be treacherous in the dark."

"I'm fine," I said. "I have someone watching over me."

The End

If you enjoyed this book, I would appreciate an honest review on Goodreads or Amazon. Thanks.

Acknowledgements:

Every book begins with an idea, sometimes multiple ideas. For this book, my sources were real history, and another book. In 1995 a microburst roared through the southern Adirondacks leaving in its wake a vast area of downed trees. A microburst is essentially a strong wind, that unlike a tornado which is circular, blows in a straight line. That microburst left a wide swath of devastation which is still visible many years later in the Adirondacks. The second idea came from a wonderful novel, *The Scent of the Missing*, by Susannah Charleson about her experience with search and rescue dogs. Put a girl who is lost in the woods together with a search and rescue dog, a good-looking forest ranger, a murder, and you have a story.

We depend on dogs, not just for their love and companionship, but to find people buried in rubble after a disaster, or in the case of this book, after they have wandered off and become lost. Like the character in this book, I have watched border collies herd sheep in the Canadian Sheep Dog Trials and been amazed at their persistence and patience.

I am also a person who has spent many years hiking, kayaking, skiing and snowshoeing in the Adirondack mountains of New York. I am a 46'r and my husband has summated all 46 peaks in summer and winter. I know about steep mountain paths, about mud, about rocks and roots underfoot, and the glorious views from the tops of the high peaks. Anyone who has spent time in these mountains knows that they are a victim of their own popularity and must, like any of our natural resources be treated with respect and care.

I am grateful to my husband Dick, and my friend, Linda Batt, who took the time to read this manuscript and offered many valuable insights into the characters and the story. I am grateful too, to you, my readers. Writing is a lonely business and it is sometimes easy to feel that no one will love the work you are creating. If you have purchased any of my books, read any of my books, or told me that you liked my books, I am deeply grateful. You, my readers, are what keep me going. Please log into my website at margueritemooers.com. This book is available on Amazon as a paperback and as a kindle e-book. It is also available on Smashwords for other e-readers. If you'd like to contact me, my e-mail is funstories043@gmail.com. Thank you.

About the Author

Before retiring, Marguerite Mooers taught inmates in a medium security prison in Upstate New York, a job which gave her lots of material for her murder mysteries. She is the author of numerous short stories and award-winning poetry, and is an enthusiastic watercolorist and watercolor teacher. Her previous novels are: *Take My Hand*, *The Shelter of Darkness*, and *A Casualty of Hope*. Find her on the web at margueritemooers.com.

Made in the USA
Columbia, SC
07 December 2017